A TEMPEST
IN HER HEART . . .

"My lord! I did not mean to imply—" she stammered in apparent innocent confusion. "I could not bear to think that we are the cause of you being forced to abandon this historic part of your birthright!"

She felt almost guilty as, to her surprise, the lord's growing anger turned swiftly to concern. Richard gently cupped her chin, forcing her to look at him. "My dear child, I will not have any of you considering yourselves burdens."

Annabelle found herself speechless. She had never had a man touch her like that. And he was being so frighteningly kind. She shielded her thoughts beneath lowered lashes, sighing in disappointment as he removed his hand.

"Now, you mustn't concern yourself further." The earl smiled in amusement at her sigh. Apparently, she felt, he was just trying to appease her . . .

Jove titles by Jacquelyn Gillis

**OTHERWISE ENGAGED
A PERFECT MISMATCH**

A Perfect Mismatch

Jacquelyn Gillis

JOVE BOOKS, NEW YORK

A PERFECT MISMATCH

A Jove Book / published by arrangement with
the author

PRINTING HISTORY
Jove edition / June 1992

All rights reserved.
Copyright © 1992 by Jacquelyn Gillis.
This book may not be reproduced in whole or in part,
by mimeograph or any other means, without permission.
For information address: The Berkley Publishing Group,
200 Madison Avenue, New York, New York 10016.

ISBN: 0-515-10893-6

Jove Books are published by The Berkley Publishing Group,
200 Madison Avenue, New York, New York 10016.
The name "JOVE" and the "J" logo
are trademarks belonging to Jove Publications, Inc.

PRINTED IN THE UNITED STATES OF AMERICA

10 9 8 7 6 5 4 3 2 1

A Perfect Mismatch

CHAPTER ONE

The man's eyes were as cold and grey as the North Sea beside him. He reined in the big stallion and it skittered a few steps as a wave crashed against the hard shales of the barren British shore. Scarcely noticing, the new Earl of Rothbury silently surveyed the expanse of his bleak heritage.

The towers of Dunne Castle jutted into the leaden evening sky like an unnatural mountain—an impregnable fortress between icy seas and endless moors.

"Why in God's holy name would anyone wish to live in such a place as this?" Richard muttered to himself.

He turned his gaze one last time to the sea, seeking the familiar white sails of the *Southwind*. However, his ship would long be on its way back to the warm tropical waters of the Caribbean with a hired master rather than her owner at the helm.

With any luck at all, he would again captain the vessel's next voyage. Richard had given himself the three months before his ship's return to put the estate in order and settle the children with a competent nanny.

Richard urged his horse forward, stoically refusing to allow his thoughts to dwell on a certain dusky-skinned beauty who would be so very disappointed when the *Southwind* docked in Jamaica without him.

Though sent some hours before him, the earl's carriage was still being unloaded in the courtyard as he rode in. An elderly servant immediately set down the piece of luggage he had been carrying and hobbled over to take the stallion's reins, struggling as the big horse tried to prance away.

"Here, old fellow." Richard leapt from the horse and gestured the man back. "Saxon's a devil to handle. Call one of the young stablehands to take him."

"Call the— Yes, milord." The man anxiously looked around, as though hoping for someone to materialize, but other than a rail-thin kitchen maid and a lad who couldn't have been more than eight years of age, the courtyard remained empty.

"Well?" Richard sighed in exasperation at the man's confusion and finally called the gaping lad over. It was cold and the hour was late. The earl was tired and totally out of patience. Where was everyone? Why were only these three out here attempting to unload the carriage? "Fetch me the stablemaster immediately, boy! And where is the butler?"

The child made an awkward bob of deference, cautiously keeping a safe distance from both the man and the horse. "Sta-stablemaster, sir?" He frantically looked at the elder servant. "Mr. Pitwick here, milord, is the—"

At that the old man stepped forward again and said, "I'm afraid, Your Lordship, there is no stablemaster—as yet. I am Alvin Pitwick, sir. I am the butler, or at least I was while His Lordship lived. Though I expect you will be bringing your own staff," he added eagerly.

"Bringing?" Richard asked, feeling the beginnings of suspicion. "What do you mean bringing? I sent my father's solicitor Hobbs out over a fortnight ago with ample funds to staff the castle and have it in readiness."

The butler shifted uneasily. "Mr. Hobbs, sir? We

haven't heard from him," he cautiously advised. "No one has arrived here, milord, except the children, of course. And even the woman who brought them refused to stay the night. She insisted on leaving with the hired equipage."

Richard stared at him. "Hired carriage? I provided Hobbs funds to purchase a traveling coach—" He suddenly stopped, realizing with disgust what had obviously occurred. That weasel Hobbs! He hadn't trusted the man from first sight. All those excuses to delay going over the records of the estate's assets until he arrived at the castle had been a ruse. Mr. Edward Hobbs was doubtless on his way to the Colonies aboard the fastest packet he could find. And if he wasn't, he'd best be! Richard grimly thought to himself.

Just then his burly coach driver came out from the castle, where he'd obviously been recruited in helping unload.

"Ben"—the earl handed the man Saxon's reins—"take this beast to the stable, assuming there is one in this rock pile! I must try to find out what the devil is going on around here. Come with me," he ordered the old butler over his shoulder as he strode into the castle.

Richard stopped at the main parlor and stood surveying it in silence until Alvin hurried up breathless beside him. "We haven't many of the rooms in readiness as of yet, milord. With only Mrs. Gavin and the maid, Kitty, and the castle being mostly closed for so very long." He anxiously hobbled over to poke up the meager coal fire. "However, I shall have Mrs. Gavin bring tea, Your Lordship. She's preparing it just now." He yanked at the scrolled bellpull.

"Thank you." Richard restrained himself from saying anything more. Glancing around the haphazardly ordered room, his eye caught a rather pathetic little flower arrangement of what appeared to be something recently plucked from the moors. "Surely, you are not telling me that this Mrs. Gavin you, that maid, and the young boy are the only staff?" He carefully kept his voice even.

"Yes, milord. Though actually Jeb, the boy, is Mrs. Gavin's grandchild. She's merely keeping him this week."

"Just three of you are attending to the castle?" Richard was sure he had misunderstood.

"Yes, milord. Of course, there are the children also. And, I must say, Miss Annabelle is such great help. I doubt we'd have managed to get by without her." He smiled reassuringly at Richard, as he surreptitiously dusted off a grand high-backed Windsor chair.

Richard cautiously sat down. "Miss Annabelle, you say? She is the governess perhaps?" he asked with some relief. Obviously, there were other persons in the employ of the estate—the old retainer was apparently just very strict in whom he defined as a servant.

The butler gave him a bit of a shocked look. "Oh no, milord, Miss Annabelle is not an—employee! She is the eldest of the children." At Richard's expression, he hurriedly added, "Of course, you have not had the opportunity to meet the children as yet, so I am sure you could not have recalled all their names." He attempted to excuse his master's embarrassing lapse.

Richard gave him a cool look. "True, I have not met the children. However, I have no difficulty in recalling two names. They are John David and Cecelia Louise. Cecelia, I presume, must have a third name she prefers to go by. Though it was my understanding she was scarcely out of leading strings. I do not understand how she could be of any great assistance with the household."

The butler opened and closed his mouth twice, his mind racing in panic. Was it possible His Lordship didn't know?

Richard rose from the chair having a very definite feeling there was something amiss. "Have I perhaps recalled the children's names in error?"

"No—no, milord, or—not those two—" the butler stammered.

"Surely you are not trying to tell me there is another child!"

"Ahem—actually Miss Annabelle is not a child, milord," Alvin hedged. "She is all of nineteen."

"Nineteen!" Richard turned in anger and stared at the old man. "My mother only died fifteen years ago! You are not presuming to suggest—"

"Oh, no. No—no, of course not, milord." In his horror Alvin dared interrupt to correct the wrong supposition. "Your father loved the countess dearly. God rest their souls. Oh, he would never—ahem—that is—Miss Annabelle is actually your step-sister. She is the older daughter of—"

"Oh, I see," Richard said. "Come to think on it, I do recall having heard that the last Lady Dunne was a widow when my father married her. It hadn't occurred to me that she might have other children. Though"—he frowned—"I fear I cannot be overly pleased to discover I've yet another ward to attend to. It was enough of a shock to find out my father had sired these two children at his age," the earl continued, almost to himself. "I suppose since this girl is of marriageable age she should not be a problem for long." Nineteen and as yet unwed? He sighed to himself. Probably a quiz! Well, with sufficient dowry any girl of family could be found some husband.

"Yes—that is, no, milord." Alvin murmured belated answers, but the earl seemed preoccupied and didn't notice. The butler had thought surely Lord Dunne would know about the second countess. Now, how in the world could he break this news? "Milord, there are other—that is, I should inform you of the additional—"

A tap at the door just then heralded Mrs. Gavin with a heavy tea tray. Alvin was only too happy to help her set it up as a momentary delay to imparting the most awkward news.

Mrs. Gavin bobbed a curtsy as she settled the tray. "'Tisn't a high tea, milord. As it being so close onto dinner, it's but scones and a few crumpets."

The gentle housekeeper looked so concerned and eager to please that Richard found himself automatically seeking to reassure her. "That will be quite sufficient, Mrs. Gavin. I am well aware I have arrived on short notice and that you have no proper staff as yet. It's a matter I shall remedy as quickly as practicable. The scones do smell delicious."

The woman glanced at Alvin and beamed. "Yes, Yer Lordship. Though you have Miss Annabelle to thank for those, milord. She has truly a light hand with the baking."

Richard forced an amicable smile though already tired of discussing the children. "I am sure she does. Pitwick, would there perhaps be a few gils of brandy in the cellars? I fear I have grown unaccustomed to this accursed cold weather and could use something a bit stronger than tea."

"Of course, milord." Thus dismissed, Alvin could scarcely tarry. With a warning glance at the housekeeper for her to follow suit, he bowed his way out.

Richard caught the glance and sighed. Doubtless, that

meant there were yet other surprises in store for him. He was aware Pitwick had been trying to elaborate on the castle's conditions, but this evening Richard was not up to hearing all of it. Tomorrow would be soon enough for him to conduct a complete tour of the estate and determine what was necessary.

Richard resettled himself before the fire, and buttered one of the flaky crumpets. That blamed Hobbs! He would pen a note to Bow Street to be put on the Royal Mail first thing tomorrow. Though it would probably be too late to catch the rogue. As it was now, he would personally have to restaff the castle along with tending to all the legal matters involved in assuming the estate. Still, he mused, the three months he had allotted should be ample time to have the estate in sufficient order to turn over to a proper steward.

Richard nodded contentedly to himself as he decided to try one of the scones. The castle was sound. Surely, the place could not be in too much disarray. And it would simply be a matter of employing servants to care for the children here rather than in the London town house.

He had intentions of using the town house himself when the *Southwind* docked at Southampton. Though Richard loved the seafaring life, he had begun to feel the pull of his homeland. And now, what with having ascended to the earldom, he would be obliged to take his place in the House of Lords to properly carry out his stewardship of Northumberland. At least one aspect of becoming guardian to the children was fortunate, Richard mused. With a much younger brother so fortuitously supplied, he would not have to suffer the usual pressure to marry and produce another heir.

By the time Alvin returned with the requested flacon, the earl had managed to talk himself into a more reasonable mood and had no intentions of letting the man ruin it with additional details. He waved the butler away as Pitwick once again attempted to correct Richard's misinterpretations concerning the children. "We shall discuss all of this on the morrow. I am sure it can wait until them. For now, I believe I shall retire to my quarters to bathe and change before dinner."

"Now? Oh, certainly, milord."

The earl raised a brow. "There is a problem?"

"No—no, milord. Of course not."

Richard considered the butler a moment before realizing the likely concern. "You may feel free to have Ben help with the hip bath and carrying the water if you wish."

"Thank you, milord. That will be quite helpful." Alvin bowed out quickly. He had best hurry or Annabelle would have used all the heated cistern water for the children.

Richard shook his head after the butler left. That poor old fellow would have probably moved the heavy bath and carried all that water himself before he'd have asked for help. But he would have sufficient staff shortly.

The earl absently reached for another pastry and was vaguely surprised to find the platter empty. Hmm. Well, at least the older girl could indeed bake.

CHAPTER TWO

Richard was surprised at the flood of nostalgic emotions he felt as he wandered about the master's suite, having long since convinced himself that the title and estate meant nothing to him. He had been sixteen when last at the castle, having come home from Eton for his mother's funeral.

Richard had left directly from school for his first seafaring position. With two elder brothers, he'd never expected to inherit and had relegated his home to the past. Thereafter, he had made a fortune building up his own fleet of swift clippers and plying the lucrative spice trade. The demands of his business had been such that he'd have but occasional contact with his homeland over the ensuing fifteen years.

A scratch at the door distracted the earl. "You may enter."

Ben shoved open the door and wheeled in an ornate hip bath, hesitating a moment as he glanced about the massive room. "Lud! Quite the place, ain't it?"

Richard smiled wryly. "A bit drafty for my taste. Though this wing was the last built and probably warmer than the rest. You may place that by the hearth over there."

He had hired Ben from a stable at Southampton and

rather enjoyed the man's casual friendliness, a trait he had dared not encourage among his ship's crew.

Ben set the bath down and peered curiously at Richard. "Don't get the feelin' you're overly pleased with yer inheritin'. I'd be thinking a bloke would be beside hi'self coming into all o'this."

The earl raised a brow at the added presumption, which, typically, Ben ignored. "But I reckon losin' your father and brother would put you off some," he mused, tossing several large lumps of coal into the iron grate.

"It would sound as if you have been quite busy gossiping in the kitchens."

Ben looked up hearing the curtness in the lord's words. "Now don't go layin' nothin' to your staff down there. Those two are 'bout as close-mouthed as they come. Too busy to talk anyway. 'Twas the innkeeper at the last cattle change what brought up the family. Country's surprised—seems as they'd thought another son was inheritin'. He die too? Now that's a pity."

"I thank you." Richard sighed, surrendering the privacy of protocol. He thought he might as well set the story straight rather than have all manner of rumors flying. "However, my brother Reynold is quite well. As he had expected our eldest brother to come into the title, he sought his own way with the Church. He simply refused to leave the priesthood to take over this heap just because Hilary was fool enough to get himself killed in a duel."

"Hmm." The man's non-comment defined his opinion without words. "Innkeeper said the villagers were hopeful the new earl would take an interest in the area. Seems once the countess died the late earl moved on into London and never came back."

Richard decided the man had strayed far enough.

"You are going to bring some water for the bath, aren't you?"

Ben simply grinned at the put-down. "Aye-aye, sir!"

Richard shook his head in wonder as Ben left. He couldn't help but like the man. Some people you just knew you could trust. He'd see if the coachman would like to stay on in his employ, Richard decided, as he loosened his cravat and tossed the annoying thing onto the huge carved bed.

Richard hadn't realized his father never returned to the castle, though he knew his mother's death had been hard on the man. He frowned at the implications, considering. Hilary had already set up his own establishment in town when their mother died. Knowing his brother's preference for the *ton* over the bucolic country life, Hilary wasn't likely to have ever made the long journey back to his birthright. For that matter, neither would have Reynold, having gone straight from seminary to a parish in Wales.

Richard faced the fact that in all probability he was going to find matters in much worse array than previously anticipated. No wonder Alvin had said the castle was mostly closed—everything had probably been under Holland covers for fifteen years. It was nothing a properly directed staff couldn't remedy, however.

The earl opened a massive armoire and was pleasantly surprised to find his own neatly folded clothing inside. The maid Kitty must be more adept than she appeared. He knew that Mrs. Gavin had been occupied in the kitchens since his arrival. He glanced around. For a limited staff, they had done rather well. At least these rooms had been turned out quite suitably. It was almost as though they had recently been in use. Perhaps he was wrong and Hilary had come up at some time.

Wondering vaguely about the condition of the rest of the castle, Richard strode over to the connecting door leading to the countess's suite.

Locked? He had never known that door to be locked. Richard smiled. Ah, he thought, they likely hadn't sufficient time to prepare the suite and had locked the door in hopes of his not discovering the state of the room. He pulled out the bronze ring of master keys picked up from his father's town house and flung open the ornate door.

"What in the—?" Richard stopped in surprise.

Startled jade green eyes flew to his, as a young woman stepped quickly away from the child whose sash she had been tying. "Run along, dear." She gestured the frightened little girl out while reaching for a robe to cover the thin chemise that was all she herself wore.

"Who in the blazes are you?" Richard ignored the child he could only assume was Cecelia Louise, as she made a frantic exit.

The young woman flushed as she quickly donned the robe. "I am Annabelle, Lord Dunne."

Annabelle? The earl stared, trying to mentally replace the expected "quiz" with this delicate beauty. So this was the older daughter. "You will be so good as to explain what you are doing in my mother's rooms—and in this state of dishabille." His eyes glanced in disdain over the thick raven hair cascading over the woman's shoulders.

Annabelle felt her temper rise. "I was dressing and, I fear, had not expected a gentleman to enter a locked door without even so much as the courtesy of a knock!"

Richard stood in shocked silence a moment. The chit had called him down? "These quarters happen to be in my suite," he finally informed her coldly. "I do believe the nurseries are still in the west wing!"

She matched him glare for glare. "Indeed, they are, sir—with windows boarded because of missing panes and fair running with rats! The children would not last a night there. This wing, in fact, is the only one even habitable in the entire castle—a matter I would think you should have considered before having the little ones sent out, even if you care nothing for the rest of us."

Richard sputtered in a mixture of fury and chagrin at her words. How dare this little witch call him down! "You will make yourself decent, miss, and report to me in my library on the hour!"

As the door slammed behind the earl, Annabelle wilted. Oh gracious, she had done it again. Mrs. Gavin had kindly warned her about her temper. But that oaf deserved it! Surely the sons had known how the late earl had abandoned them to their own devices all of these years. And now even that miserly stipend Hobbs sent up quarterly had stopped. Of course, it wasn't really old Lord Dunne's fault. He had been more than generous until his mind started to go and that Lady Matilda got her wretched claws into him. But now what would happen to the children?

Would this new earl merely turn them all out? Surely not, when at least the twins and Cathy were actually his blood. But then again, the earl's sons had totally ignored her mother's part of their family all these years. Apparently, the second countess wasn't of high enough birth for their exalted notice!

"Miss Annabelle!"

Annabelle turned with a sigh as yet again her door burst open, though this time it was the hall door and only Kitty confronted her, wringing her hands. "What is it,

Kitty?" Annabelle forgot her other problems at the girl's frantic face.

"It's Master John, miss. Oh, do please hurry. Please," Kitty cried grabbing Annabelle's hand and tugging her on.

"What? What has happened to Master John?" Annabelle quickly discarded the robe and donned an old morning dress over her chemise as the girl managed to sob out the newest disaster.

"His foot, miss. He got hold of the ax. He was trying to help with the fire logs. Oh, miss—it's blood everywhere!"

"Oh, dear heaven, not the ax!"

Annabelle grabbed her worn woolen cape, merely tossing her hair off her shoulders as she ran down the stairs.

The sight that met her in the kitchens was beyond enough to cause a more faint-hearted woman to collapse into the vapors. Blood was indeed everywhere. Mrs. Gavin was wailing and Alvin was frantically trying to still the thrashing child to determine the extent of the injury.

"Here, darling." Annabelle soothed the boy with forced calm and finally managed to quiet him enough to remove his small boot. Though a serious wound, she was relieved. "It is not as bad as it could have been. But I do think we had best get you to Dr. Wattle, dear."

She gestured to Ben, who had just returned from delivering his lordship's bath water.

"Miss? What is—?"

"Would you be good enough to drive us into the village, Ben? It's just a quarter hour across the moor."

The coachman, who had taken quite a fancy to this bizarre family, readily agreed without a thought of obtaining his lordship's permission. "Come along, lad." He easily scooped up John David.

"I had best go with you." Alvin shrugged into his heavy coat. "Doc Wattle's not always easy to locate."

"Thank you," Annabelle said gratefully. "I'm sorry to be leaving you with this mess, Mrs. Gavin. We'll return as soon as we can."

Richard was stripped and about to step into his bath when he heard the clatter of hooves across the courtyard. He pulled back the draperies just in time to glimpse a raven-haired lass leap into his carriage with someone else before it careened off through the crumbling barbican. Good God, had that wench decided to run away rather than face him?

"There is definitely more going on here than meets the eye," Richard muttered to himself as he climbed into the fast-cooling hip tub, "but I shall get to the bottom of it and soon!"

A girlish giggle interrupted his irate soliloquy. Richard spun about to meet a pair of merry green eyes set in an impish little face peeking at him from the adjoining day room. Just as suddenly as she'd appeared, the child vanished with a flash of homespun skirts. He started to stand up to give chase before recalling his state of undress.

"What in Satan's hell is going on around here?" Richard looked at the bellpull across the room in exasperation. Well, surely Pitwick would be up shortly.

That wasn't the same child Annabelle had had with her earlier. He hadn't seen much of the new little girl, but the first child had long light-colored hair, not that mop of ebony curls or those green eyes—so much like Annabelle's.

"Good lord!" A thought occurred to Richard. Was this why everyone was acting so strangely? Could this be what Alvin had been trying to tell him all along? It did fit. Perhaps this explained why no one had heard anything about an older daughter of Lady Matilda and why someone with her looks was unwed at nineteen. Had she been banished to Northumbria enceinte? Could that have been what she meant when she said he didn't care about the rest of them? And now, rather than face him, had she run away and left the child? This was all beyond enough!

Richard hastily finished his bath, then angrily yanked at the bellpull. The deteriorated tapestry strip fell in dusty folds at his feet. "Oh damn!"

Thoroughly exasperated, the earl dried himself, but by the time he was dressed he had changed his mind about confronting the elderly butler. No, the old man and housekeeper were clearly not at fault. They had probably assumed he knew—which of course he should have, had that blamed Hobbs done his duty.

He would have that wench brought back and made to face him as she should, Richard determinedly told himself as he struggled with the unaccustomed chore of tying the fanciful folds of his cravat.

He caught a slight movement in the mirror and stared in shock as a pale little figure in a long white gown silently flitted across the room behind him and into the hall.

"What the—?" Richard spun to the hall door but the apparition was nowhere in sight. "Now that was neither the imp with black curls nor the child who was with Annabelle!" he exclaimed aloud not seeing Kitty approach.

"Milord?"

The earl started in surprise at the voice behind him.

"Uh, Yer Lordship," Kitty began again in concern at his stormy look. "Mr. Pitwick said I was to bring up more coal." She displayed as evidence the skuttle she carried.

"Who was that child who just came into this hall?"

"S-Sir?" Kitty had not seen Elizabeth slip into the next room, and had been firmly warned by Alvin not to mention anything about the other children until he could explain to the earl himself. "I didn't see no—"

"Of course you did!" Richard was altogether out of patience with this obvious charade. "A thin girl with pale hair in a white gown? She just now came out of this doorway and then vanished!"

Kitty turned white as a sheet at his words. "Va-Vanished, milord?" Her Tim had warned her that Dunne Castle was haunted and she shouldn't go all the way up there alone! And everyone had heard the whispered tales of the Black Earl's poor murdered daughter Melissa. Tim had even shown her the old moss-covered grave in the village kirk yard. "Melissa Cynthia Dunne, born 1618, died 1623" was the old grey stone's inscription.

"Well, did you see her?"

"See Mel—Melissa?" The girl quaked in horror as her mental fantasy took firm hold.

"Yes, Melissa, I suppose," Richard acknowledged in continued exasperation. "Why the blazes can't I ever get a sensible answer? Where is Melissa?"

The coal scuttle rattled ominously. "She—she's dead. She's a ghost, milord!" Kitty cried out, dropped the coal skuttle, and fled down the stairs.

The earl stood dumbfounded, unable to resist a cautious glance into the shadowy hall behind him before he brought his mind to order.

"Pitwick!" The lord's voice thundered through the

castle sending the little scullery maid tumbling down the last few steps. Quite sure the lord's yell meant the end of him at the hands of some dread horror, the maid dashed into her room and dove headlong beneath her bed.

Even Mrs. Gavin in the kitchens below heard the lord's bellowing, but having a pretty good notion what it meant, wisely decided to take herself and little Jeb well out of reach of the lord's ire. She'd intended to clean up the bloody mess from John David's foot, but hustled Jeb out to the relative safety of the poultry house on the contrived excuse that she had to gather eggs for the morrow. Alvin had explained that the earl apparently knew nothing about his father's other family. And she wasn't about to assume the task of telling him. Alvin could handle it when he got back.

All the remaining children managed to disappear in the inexplicable way children can on hearing an angry adult. The furious lord now found himself storming through an apparently empty castle.

"Pitwick? Mrs. Gavin? Ben?"

Nothing but echoes answered Richard's shouts, nor did any of the few working bellpulls in the vacant rooms bring a response.

Muttering curses, Richard finally condescended to go down to the kitchen himself to worm them out. It was clear that they all were trying to hide something from him.

Richard's mood waxed no better as he stumbled down a poorly lit servants' stairway to the main kitchen. It was fully dark outside. Why weren't there lamps lit in these halls?

"Mrs.—" Richard shoved open the kitchen door and abruptly stopped at the scene. Blood was everywhere—

all over the floor. Richard walked over in shock to find a bloody hand ax lying ominously to the side.

"Good God!" he gasped. "Have they all been attacked by some madman?"

CHAPTER THREE

Terrance, with the usual adventurous nature of an eight-year-old, carefully slipped from his favored hiding place under the stairwell after the earl passed by and silently followed. In happy anticipation he watched the earl, concealed behind the kitchen door Richard had left open.

The boy had to stifle his giggles seeing the big man's look of horror as he viewed the kitchen scene. Terry, of course, knew all about John David's accident as he and Thomas, his twin, had also been involved in the attempted wood chopping, though they had sworn John David to secrecy.

He and Thomas were the most eager of the children to meet this new "big brother." They had been sorely disappointed when Annabelle and Mr. Pitwick had explained that the new earl didn't know about them as yet and that they would have to stay out of sight until proper explanations could be made.

Posh, Terry had decided, having sized the man up with childish optimism. He looked like a good cove. Surely, he would be pleased to find he had two more brothers. After all, he and Thomas had been delighted when John David had shown up. Why, he probably wouldn't even mind the girls, either. Cathy and Liz weren't bad 'uns—for females, of course.

Terry had just about made up his mind to present himself to this wonderful new brother when Richard sensed he was being watched. Still harboring thoughts of some lurking madman, Richard suddenly grabbed a handy meat cleaver and flung the door back—revealing the now-terrified lad.

"Yiiii! Don't hack me!" Terry screamed.

As the lord gaped in astonishment, the boy ducked under his upraised arm and skittered back beneath the stairwell.

"Wait, come back here!" the earl demanded, throwing down the cleaver in disgust as he headed after the boy.

"No!" Thomas, who had been watching the scene from behind a woodbox in the hallway, jumped up to save his brother. As Richard turned to him, Thomas forgot bravery and took off through the kitchens.

Richard glanced first in the direction the boy had run and then back at the stairwell. "Jove! Am I losing my mind?" He was certain he had distinctly seen that lad duck beneath the stairwell. Now just how in the dickens had he managed to get back behind him? Where in the devil were all these children coming from?

Just then he heard a slight bump and he quietly crept up on the staircase. Indeed, someone must still be under there!

As the earl eased up the stairs, Terry decided to risk a glance out, thinking perhaps the lord had chased after Thomas.

"Ah-ha, now I have you!" Richard grabbed the boy triumphantly by the collar and Terry let out a loud squawk of surprise.

"Be quiet, I am not going to—" However, Richard

was unable to complete his sentence as a small whirling dervish appeared from nowhere to attack his knees.

"Leave my brother alone. Let him go! Let him go!" cried the frantic little Catherine.

"Get 'um, Caffy," a yet smaller elfin child happily lisped from a safe vantage point on the stairs.

The earl determinedly kept hold of the one lad he'd captured and still managed to grab the tiny flailing fists of the dark-haired pugilist. "Stop that this instant and be still, you two!"

"Let them go."

The small voice was quite firm. Richard was taken aback to find it came from his earlier "ghost"—a young girl of perhaps ten years of age who walked down the stairway gripping a huge flintlock blunderbuss aimed in the general direction of his chest.

"Good going, Lizzie!" Thomas complimented her as he skipped back out of the kitchens. "Don't let 'im hurt 'em."

Richard blinked and had to look back down to where he still held Terry. There were two of them!

"Let them go or I shall be forced to use this!"

The earl kept his composure as the antique weapon had doubtless not been fired in a century or more. "Very well. You may lower the weapon, but please do not run off again. I have no intention of harming any of you."

"He attacked me with the meat cleaver!" Terry angrily accused. "Shoot him, Lizzie. Go ahead, shoot him!"

"I do apologize for frightening you." Richard tried to calm the lad. "I was not going to attack you. It's just that I saw all that blood—and then there was the blood-stained ax. I feared perhaps some madman was loose in the castle. Whatever happened in the kitchen?"

The children giggled.

"A madman, indeed! What a gudgeon! 'Twas only John David. He chopped his foot," Thomas casually explained. "Annie had to take him in to Doc."

Richard overlooked the child calling him a gudgeon. "John David injured? Why has no one informed me of this?"

"Oh, he'll be all right," Terry added consolingly. "I saw it—none of the toes came off or anything. You needn't get all in a tither."

Richard blanched slightly at the "toes" remark. "You realize that child is my brother. Someone should have come to me if he was injured!"

"Well, we're your brothers, too," Terry piped up, forgetting that it was a secret, "and you chopped at me with a cleaver!"

"I most assuredly did no such—what do you mean you're my brothers?" Richard stared at the twins aghast.

"Oh, Thomas!" Elizabeth finally put down the rusty firearm to chastise her brother. "You weren't supposed to tell about us!"

"Us?" Richard began to feel slightly faint as he looked over the seeming sea of expectant childish faces. "Who—who exactly are you children?" he finally managed.

"Well, I suppose it's out now anyway." The older girl, Elizabeth, stepped down from her perch and offered the blunderbuss to Richard, taking charge. "I am Elizabeth, my lord, and this is Catherine." She drew the two younger girls over, and after a nudge they each made a giggling curtsy. "This is Cecelia. We are your sisters and the twins are Terrance and Thomas, your brothers, along with Master John David, of course."

The earl opened his mouth, but when no words came forth he closed it again.

The stalwart Terrance took this silence as acceptance. "Now see there, I told you all he was a right cove. He doesn't mind having us—"

"Terry, Annie told you not to use those cant phrases," Liz corrected her brother primly.

"Ahem, I am afraid I do not quite understand," Richard finally managed carefully. "You are my sisters and brothers? All of you?"

"Yes. So we've been told. Annie, too, of course." Thomas stepped up beside his twin, and having dispensed with that subject moved on to one more interesting. "Mr. Pitwick said you are a seaman. That you have your own ship. Are you a pirate?" he asked hopefully.

"Of course he's not a pirate!" Liz glared at her brother. "He's a lord. Lords are never pirates—they are privateers."

Richard blinked. "If you don't mind. I was told Lady Matilda only had two children, and Annabelle, who I have discovered was her daughter from a previous marriage."

"Annie, Lady Matilda's daughter? Whoever told you that? Annie's our sister. Lady Matilda was the mother of Cecelia and John David. Our mother was Elsbeth Ashley, until she married Lord Dunne," Elizabeth enlightened him.

The earl drew a deep breath. "My father, Lord Dunne, was married twice?"

Elizabeth considered seriously a moment. "Three times, I should think, counting your mother."

"Oh, yes. Of course." Richard tried to keep his thoughts rational. "You said your mother was—?"

"Elsbeth Ashley." Elizabeth sighed as though explaining to someone a bit slower than herself. "Mother already had Annie and me when she met Lord Dunne. Our father was Major Seymour Ashley. Mama said he was killed with Wellond— Wesling— Fighting the evil French," she finally amended, "and because she was lonely and wanted more children Lord Dunne married her. Lord Dunne is also the father of Cathy and the twins." Elizabeth paused for breath. "Doesn't anyone tell you anything?"

"Apparently not," Richard admitted a bit grimly.

"Hmm. Well, Mr. Pitwick did say you were mostly at sea."

Richard raised a brow at the phrase, but the child paid no heed. "When Mama died, Lord Dunne sent us from London to live here at the castle. He said he would join us but he never did. Annie said it was because he married Lady Matilda, and new wives don't want a bunch of children around." She hesitated, worried. "Do you have a wife?"

Richard looked down as five small faces turned to him in sudden anxiety. "No. As yet, I haven't a wife."

"Good." Elizabeth radiated a beautiful smile, the matter obviously settled. "If you will please excuse us, my lord, I really must get Cathy and Cecelia ready for bed before Annie returns and finds them still up and about."

The earl nodded a bemused permission as the older girl herded her giggling charges up the stairs. Shaking his head in wonder, he glanced back down to discover the twins were apparently not under the same bedtime curfew. Both boys beamed as he noticed them again.

"I know you couldn't speak about it with the girls around, sir, but now that they've gone you can tell us your seafaring adventures."

"Just how many ships have you sunk?" Thomas excitedly asked.

"Boys!" Mrs. Gavin had finally regained courage to return and was shocked at finding the twins with the earl.

"What are you two doing out of your beds? Miss Annabelle will have your very hides!"

Apparently, Miss Annabelle's name was enough to strike fear in even the most staunch of hearts and the two quickly darted up the stairs after their sisters.

"Milord, on the boys, well, Mr. Pitwick wished to speak—"

"I have met the children, Mrs. Gavin," Richard informed her coolly, none too pleased at his servants' part in the deception, "and, I might add, they have explained their relationship."

The housekeeper nervously wrung her hands. "They did? You met all the children?"

"All?" Richard felt another brief rush of panic. "I met five—I certainly hope to high heaven that is all."

"Well, not counting Master John David and Miss Annabelle," Mrs. Gavin said cautiously, and the earl let out a sigh of relief.

"Of course. I will discuss this matter of the children with you and Pitwick at a more opportune time. For now, I would like to know what has happened to John David. How badly was he injured?"

"Oh, it were a bad cut right enough, milord, but the tyke'll be all right. Miss Annabelle and Alvin, they got your man Ben to take the young master in to Doc Wattle. You needn't fear he's one of those cuppin' leaches, the Doc. He'll cleanse the tyke and bandage him proper."

"Perhaps I should ride in and see to them myself."

"As you wish, of course Yer Lordship, but I shouldn't have you bother. You'd likely pass them. I'd expect they should be back most any time now. The village is but a bit down the road." She hopefully glanced toward the still-empty courtyard, uncomfortable in her sole audience with the earl.

Richard considered. She was probably right. Not to mention the fact that he suddenly found himself quite tired. The preliminary signs of an impending headache made a night ride decidedly unappealing.

"Very well, Mrs. Gavin. You will immediately notify me upon their return. Now, if you would be so good, I would appreciate having a decanter of brandy brought to the library."

"Yes, milord."

"Some very strong brandy," he quietly added as he strode off.

CHAPTER FOUR

Richard sank down heavily in his father's leather chair and stared unseeing at the remaining embers of the library fire.

Seven children.

Distractedly, he ran a hand through his thick, dark hair. Had his father married twice more? Who was this Elsbeth woman? Ashley? He had never heard the name. Apparently, as her first husband was of rank in Wellington's army, he could have been a peer, though most like not of much title.

Seven children.

Nonetheless, he wouldn't allow it to change anything. It would simply take a bit more planning—and perhaps a larger purse. Fortunately, his pockets were plump enough to manage without strain.

"Yes, come in." He stopped his thoughts as Mrs. Gavin entered bearing a slightly tarnished tray with the requested brandy and glasses. "Good heavens, woman, I didn't expect you to bring this yourself. I know you are trying to clean up and prepare a meal. Why didn't you send the maid?"

"It's of no matter, milord." Mrs. Gavin sat the tray down. "Though I do fear, what with everything else, dinner is getting later and later. And I don't know what has become of that Kitty. I can't seem to find her anywhere."

"Oh, Kitty," Richard started guiltily. "Well, I might have had a hand in her disappearance."

"You, sir?" The woman glanced up, startled.

Richard chuckled. "Perhaps quite inadvertently. I saw one of the children—Elizabeth, I believe—upstairs . . ." He briefly explained to Mrs. Gavin the chain of events. "It would appear Kitty thought I had seen the ghost of some past resident she called Melissa. Does any of this mean anything to you?"

Mrs. Gavin sniffed in annoyance. "Bit of fustian is all, milord. A tale the village lads scare silly girls with. There is a grave in the village kirk yard of one Melissa Dunne. Poor mite what died ages ago. Somehow the story is come that she still walks the castle at night," she continued, making a sweeping gesture with her hand.

Richard smiled. "Well, your Kitty almost convinced me. No doubt she's somewhere in hiding after I told her I'd seen this Melissa."

"Probably's locked up in her sleepin' room." The housekeeper frowned, not at all amused by the ridiculous goings-on and the extra work it was causing her. "I'll send Jeb to fetch her. Maybe if he tells her it was just Miss Elizabeth you saw . . ." The old woman headed to the door still muttering to herself.

"Mrs. Gavin."

The woman stopped in concern. "Beggin' your pardon, Yer Lordship, I didn't mean no—"

"No, that is all right." Richard soothed her fear that she was about to get called down for disrespect—though under normal conditions hers was not at all the type attitude he would have tolerated. "I am aware this whole evening has been an impossible strain with such a small staff. You may dispense with any formal meal. I shall be quite content, under the circumstances, with a light supper of whatever you have already prepared. You may bring a tray here to the library. On the morrow, perhaps Pitwick will be able to bring some village women out to help."

Mrs. Gavin bobbed a grateful curtsy. "Thank ye, milord. I must admit to being a bit pressed to put a proper meal together, with only what we have. There is the steak and kidney pie, and venison of course—and we've been fortunate with the kitchen's garden this spring—"

Richard politely stemmed the woman's lengthy explanations. "I'm sure that will be fine."

Once the housekeeper left, the earl thoughtfully sipped his brandy. To hear the woman go on you would almost think there had been no funds at all sent to the castle!

The Rothbury earldom had always been prosperous from its enormous size alone. The earl opened the cabinet that held the account books, and shook a fine layer of dust from the top volume before opening it up.

Richard had been involved in deciphering the unformed writing for some time when he was interrupted.

"Milord?"

Richard hadn't heard Alvin's tap on the door and turned to find the very distraught looking butler waiting at the entry.

"Come in, Pitwick," Richard tersely advised. "Is John David all right?"

"Yes, Your Lordship. The young master is fine. Doc—the village physician—bandaged his foot and said but to keep it clean of corruption and it should leave naught but a thin scar. The boy was asleep, so Miss

Annabelle has taken him on up to his bed, if that be all right, sir."

Richard nodded. "I suppose Mrs. Gavin has told you I have, shall we say, discovered my father's other family?"

"Yes, milord. Milord, I did try—I mean to say, at first, I just naturally thought that you knew about Mrs. Ashley—the second countess—but then—"

"I understand, Pitwick." The earl stopped the man's rather frantic explanation. "It is a matter I certainly should have known about it. However, I fear I was never close enough to Hilary to correspond and, of course, with his priesthood Reynold had no time to track me down. Doubtless, he assumed my father or his steward kept in touch with me."

Richard poured himself a second brandy before gesturing to the account books he had been studying. "For the moment we shall dispense with the matter of the children. I find myself more concerned with the state of these accounts."

"Accounts, sir?" Alvin glanced nervously at the dusty books. "I fear, sir, Mrs. Gavin has not dusted properly—"

"I am not referring to their physical state! I am concerned with the entries. With the lack of a steward, it falls to you as butler to enter monies received and their disbursements. This last entry—and an apparently incomplete one at that—is a small sum received well over a year ago."

Alvin peered down at the indicated figure in confusion. "Yes, milord. That is my entry. I fear my penmanship is not rightly—"

"Penmanship!" Richard sighed. "Pitwick, where are the entries since this date?"

"S-Sir. There have been no funds to enter."

"What?"

"That is God's holy truth, milord," Alvin assured him, fearing the earl might have thought him a thief. "That last year—well, the monies sent became less and less. Mr. Givins, the late earl's steward of many years, was replaced by Mr. Hobbs a bit over two years ago. After that, as you will see here, milord, the amounts as well as the correspondence with London went down, till finally they ceased altogether. I'm sure if you inquire of this Hobbs, sir, he'll explain. I believe you said he should be coming up."

Richard stared at the dusty ledger book with dawning understanding. "No. I seriously doubt we shall ever see Mr. Hobbs again, unless Bow Street can find him!"

"B-Bow Street, sir?"

Richard ignored Alvin's question. "Am I to understand that you and Mrs. Gavin have been functioning here at the castle for over a year with no monies?"

"Well—yes, milord. Of course, we have had the kitchen garden and the estate livestock to draw upon from time to time. And we have traded out quite a bit with the villagers—"

"What of the home farms?"

"Their shares have been going straight to London, milord, ever since the late earl moved. The staff here, sir, didn't even know of the earl's remarriage until after Lady Elsbeth's demise when the earl sent the children up." Alvin reached for the books. "If I may, sir?"

At Richard's nod, he turned back several pages. "Here, milord. The earl sent monies to begin re-staffing the castle. It was expected he would be coming himself, but that was when he met the Lady Matilda. The funds continued being quite sufficient, as you shall see, until about five years ago. As the monies decreased we had to lay off staff. I did write, sir, to London, but there was never a reply—not one line."

At the earl's foreboding silence, Alvin nervously shifted. "I swear, Your Lordship, on my mother's blessed name, neither I nor Mrs. Gavin would take funds from the accounts, milord!"

Richard absently patted the man on the shoulder. "I did not think you had, Pitwick. It would appear, in fact, that I am quite in debt to you for staying and caring for five children under the circumstances."

Alvin smiled in relief. "The children were no problem, milord. They are all such a delight. Miss Annabelle pretty well took over their care once their governess left. As for Mrs. Gavin and me—well, we didn't really have anywhere else to go. Nay, no one else would want me at my age—and Mrs. Gavin's grown children are in the village, so she liked staying on close."

"Well, you may both be assured you will be fully reimbursed back wages plus bonuses as soon as I can manage to sort out this mess."

"Thank ye, milord." Alvin hesitated. "Miss Annabelle had mentioned you wished to see her, sir. She was concerned that she had angered you by staying in the countess's rooms. I must apologize, milord, for that arrangement must be laid at my door. As we hadn't heard from His Lordship in so very long—and the master's wing being the only one in good repair—I fear I've allowed Miss Annabelle and the children the run of those quarters."

The earl smiled wryly. "Apparently, that accounts for their continually popping in at the oddest times."

"Popping in, sir?" Alvin was unaware of all that had transpired earlier that evening.

"Never you mind. You may, however, advise Annabelle our meeting may wait until the morrow. I have quite enough here to occupy my evening."

CHAPTER FIVE

The following morning found the earl up at dawn to seek out the butler for a tour of the castle. Having pored over the estate accounts well into the night, Richard had very grim expectations of how he would find his inheritance.

Other than the few rooms currently in use, it was soon evident that even the newer wing would require a major turning out as well as the replacement of most of the draperies and upholstery. Richard was pleased to find that the construction was yet sound enough to keep out the elements and the worst of the vermin. But not even this wing could be counted as a proper abode for the Earl of Rothbury's family without immediate attention.

After the two hours required to survey the first wing, the earl found his hand aching from writing the long list of needed repairs. He absently massaged it. Ever since a nasty slash from the broken edge of a falling yardarm, he had had difficulty writing for long periods of time.

"I will breakfast now. And afterward, we shall continue with the remainder of the castle," the earl advised Alvin.

"Yes, milord," the butler managed faintly, while still trying to catch his breath after following his master's long strides through the endless halls and up steep stairways.

Richard glanced at the old man in chagrin. "It shall not be necessary for you to accompany me on the balance of the tour. However, I fear this accursed hand is giving out on me. I must give it a rest."

At the butler's concerned look he explained. "It is just an old wound, but it does interfere somewhat with my writing. I would have a steward here for any such duties, if that rogue Hobbs had done as instructed—" Richard paused as a sudden, very satisfying idea occurred to him. "Just now all I need is assistance with some simple notetaking. Would you know whether the older girl, Annabelle, is reasonably good with her letters?"

The butler looked at him in surprise. "Of course, milord. Miss Annabelle is quite learned. In fact, she had completely taken over as tutor for all the children. Why, even in her spare time—not that there is much—you will always find her poring over some of those old volumes from your library."

"Very well," Richard acknowledged shortly, annoyed at finding he had once again stirred the pot of this presumed paragon's virtues. "You may have her await me after breakfast. She will accompany me through the rest of the castle and take notes." Though he would normally never have considered subjecting a young lady to an arduous day of touring the empty wings, Richard smugly determined that the time under his tutelage would supply an obviously needed redress of that chit's manners.

"I am sure Miss Annabelle will be pleased to help." Alvin felt a faint twinge of conscience on consigning the girl to trudging through a cold, musty and vermin-inhabited castle, but stoically determined that she could manage it a lot better than he.

* * *

"Alvin!" Annabelle protested when the butler informed her of Lord Dunne's wishes. "You know I have the twins' Latin recitals this morning—and Cathy's lesson. And John David is still much too fussy with his foot for Mrs. Gavin to handle—not to mention that I have not even begun the baking for this evening." Annabelle frowned, thinking the man probably didn't need her at all anyway. Making her traipse through rat-infested hallways with him was doubtless just his way of getting even with her for daring to speak back to him last evening.

"Missy." Alvin reverted to using her childhood name in his distress. "I am only relating that which His Lordship has requested."

"I know." Annie sighed, realizing she was trapped. "I just don't know how I can manage to—"

"There now, Miss Annabelle," the housekeeper broke in considerately. "I can let Kitty off her other chores to watch after the little ones. Alvin can carry Master John down here, and I'll set him up on a pallet right out there in the kitchen garden. It's fair and bright today—the sunshine will do him a world of good. I'll get my Jeb to keep him amused. As for the twins, I can't quite imagine those two fussing at missing a lesson!"

Annabelle smiled weakly. "Thank you, Mrs. Gavin. Perhaps I can be back in time to help with the baking."

"Now don't you go botherin' yourself about that none. I can manage. And if His Lordship has to make do with my scones, it'll be his due for taking you off!"

The idea of the haughty Lord Dunne at the mercy of Mrs. Gavin's infamously bad scones brightened Annabelle's mood a little. "Well, at least once this high and mighty earl sees the shape the rest of his castle is in, he will probably quickly take himself back off to London!"

"Why, Miss Annabelle!" The housekeeper looked at her in surprise. "I don't believe I ever heard you say an unkind word about anyone before. Whatever has set you so against His Lordship? Mr. Pitwick and I were just sayin' how understandin' the man has been, especially considerin' the circumstances he's come to find."

Annabelle wasn't about to relate the embarrassing episode in the countess's suite, or the effect the earl's eyes raking over her in such disdain had on her morale. "I'm sorry. You are right, of course. I suppose I am just tired. John David allowed me very little sleep last evening."

"You poor pet," Mrs. Gavin clucked. "Now you run on upstairs and put on something warmer for those cold hallways. And do wear a shawl, mind you. I'll send Kitty up with a tea tray as I doubt you've stopped for a bite all morning."

In her room, Annabelle studied her small choice of gowns in dismay. It rarely even occurred to her to worry about what she wore, but somehow she was reluctant to appear before the earl in her usual faded and much-mended morning dresses. Not that it mattered. After all, he had made his opinion of her rather clear on their first meeting.

Annabelle pulled out a heavier gown from the back of the armoire and slipped it on—at least she could be warm. She stared at her reflection in the canted pier glass. Heavens, she hadn't realized how much weight she had lost since she'd worn the gown last winter. To her own critical eye she appeared thin and haggard. She sighed in dejection as she braided her heavy raven locks, never even seeing the beautiful bone structure and quite lovely eyes in the reflection in the mirror.

"Why are you sad, Annie?" The worried little voice from her doorway made Annabelle turn with a forced smile.

"I'm not sad, Ceci."

"Yes, you are sad," the child persisted. "Annie, has something bad happened?"

"No, darling." Annabelle gathered up the child for a consoling hug. "Actually, I was just brushing this awful dark hair of mine and wishing it was a lovely gold like yours," she teased, running her brush playfully through the girl's locks to distract her.

"I like your hair better." Cecelia reached up to touch the crown of braid Annie had wound about her head "But it's prettier when it's not in this knot thing," she added with innocent candor.

Annabelle laughed. "Well, I'm afraid at my age it isn't considered proper to go about with hair dangling loose to one's waist. Now aren't you supposed to be in the classroom studying your alphabet?"

"I don't 'member the alphabets!" the little girl grumbled. "Will you show me again?"

"Now I won't be able to help you today; but here, I can write them out for you." Annabelle took the notebook and pen she had ready for her tour with the earl and quickly outlined the letters. "There now, you can trace over these until you learn them."

The child dejectedly accepted the paper. "Why aren't you coming with me? You aren't leaving, are you, Annie?"

Annabelle's heart constricted on discovering the child's fear of another change. At only four years of age, Cecelia had already lost both her father and mother and had been moved far away from her only home.

"No, darling, of course I'm not leaving," she carefully

reassured her, and was pleased to see the child relax. "I merely have to help show the earl around the castle today."

"What's an—arl?" The girl looked at her in confusion.

Annabelle grinned as she led the child to the school room. "Earl, dear. You met him last evening, remember? He is your older brother."

"That's what John David said," the child skeptically allowed, "but I never saw a brother that big."

Annabelle was still chuckling over that statement as she headed down the stairs to find the subject of her amusement impatiently awaiting her at the landing.

"Am I perhaps taking you from some more pleasant diversion?" he coolly quipped with a meaningful glance at his pocket watch.

Annabelle hid her irritation under lowered lashes. "I apologize, my lord. I must admit I took a moment to help your sister Cecelia with her alphabet on my way to take notes for you. Ceci seemed to have forgotten her letter shapes." She innocently smiled up at him. "This is perhaps a problem that runs in your family?"

The earl was momentarily so distracted by the full force of those emerald eyes that her words took several seconds to sink in.

Annabella was rewarded by seeing his countenance then turn a dark red.

"You shall quickly find, miss, that I am not a man it is wise to goad," he growled. "I requested your assistance because it is difficult to me to write for long periods with this blasted hand!"

Annabelle stared in chagrin at the heavy, jagged scar across the back of the earl's right hand. "Oh, Lord Dunne! I am truly sorry! I did not realize—Oh, sir—"

The earl was surprised to see very real tears glistening in the girl's eyes. "I must confess, I had—I had actually suspected your summons was merely to repay me for my—my remark of last evening. I never even imagined that you—that you were truly in need."

The earl found himself speechless at her sudden onslaught of guilt. Annabelle took his silence as further condemnation. "I apologize to you for last evening, also, my lord. I had assumed that you knew of the conditions we had been living with here at the castle and that you merely didn't care. Alvin has, of course, now explained that you truly knew nothing of our mother's marriage to the late earl."

"Your apologies are accepted." Richard managed evenly, dismissing his fear that the girl would determine his truer motives in asking for her assistance. "Perhaps we can begin again on a better understanding all around?"

"Thank you, my lord!"

Richard looked away from her grateful smile. "I am sure I can manage the castle tour now without your aid—" He tried to get out of the rather ungentlemanly position, but Annabelle would have none of it.

"Oh no, please, my lord. You must allow me to help, as I would feel ever so badly if you didn't."

CHAPTER SIX

The earl led Annabelle from the west wing into the great west tower. "This tower was strictly defensive. Down here were numerous armories. The stairs rise to the covered walks of battlements now abandoned," Richard explained as they traversed the huge vacant round room with vaulted ceilings.

Annabelle clutched her woolen shawl about her against the cold, near-constant sea wind whistling like the ghosts of arrows through the tower loophole slits and the rows of machicolations overhead.

"My brothers and I used these towers as indoor playrooms when we dared not venture outside." Richard smiled, seeming not to even notice the raw, cold wind. "Many an invader met his fate at our hands."

She was relieved when he finally strode on across the tower to the massive iron-plated oaken double doors leading to the east wing. Annabelle's relief, however, was short-lived as he struggled to open the rusted lock.

The earl muttered an expletive before recalling his companion. "My apologies. I simply cannot believe my father never had his steward come up to check on repairs."

Annabelle sighed in relief when the ancient key partially opened the lock, but again it caught and refused to give in to his efforts.

Richard finally noticed her shudder in the cold wind. "Oh, blast," he muttered, and forcefully bore his shoulder into the doors, causing the metal of the corroded hasp to crumble into pieces.

"Well, you'll not want this wing separated anyway," Annabelle said consolingly. "Removing the doors would allow easy access to this entire section of the castle."

"True, but I am not so sure any of this will be salvable. It would appear there has been extensive leakage. Make a note to have roofers check this wing. No, you may just as well have them inspect the entire castle."

Entering the wide hallway, he glanced about and remarked, "These rugs will all have to be replaced."

Annabelle gave him a surprised glance as he casually dismissed the lovely thick Persian runners that covered most of the dark oak flooring, because of the mildew darkening their intricate patterns. The earl however didn't notice her look as he turned to open the nearest door.

"Draperies, rugs and bed hangings—this settee should be recovered," he continued.

Annabelle had to write quickly to keep up as the earl strode through the room flipping up Holland covers, rapping at furniture for soundness, and kicking aside scattered rugs to check the flooring underneath.

"If you will, you might label the rooms," he advised with a glance at her notes. "I suppose we shall need measurements for all of these draperies and such to order them," the earl mused, more to himself than Annabelle.

"No, actually I should think, as it seems there is going to be considerable replacement necessary, that it would be more frugal to buy material in bolts and have a seamstress come to the castle to sew," Annabelle advised him, unthinking. At his sharp look, she feared she had again annoyed him. "I am sorry, my lord. I did not mean to—"

"Not at all." He waved aside her protest. "That is a splendid idea. It should cut the expense by more than half. Excellent." He nodded, considering her with a rather surprised expression. "You may feel free to make whatever suggestions you deem wise. I must admit refurbishing a home is not an area in which I have previous experience."

"If you are sure you don't mind." Annabelle took him at his word and eagerly glanced around. "I do believe you are planning to replace considerable things that should be saved." The earl's lips ominously tightened, and Annabelle quickly added, "Please, sir. That was not intended as a criticism. It is only that you would, of course, not be familiar with the more mundane housekeeping matters such as the fact that mildew can be rather easily removed with a bit of lemon juice and adequate sunshine."

He looked at her suspiciously, quite aware that her words were very carefully chosen to placate him. "Hmm. Do continue."

"Well, I was merely thinking it would be a shame to discard all of these lovely Persian rugs. I should think they would be of value," she cautiously added.

Richard stooped down and curiously touched the black spots marring the rug he stood on. "You are saying all of this can be removed?"

"Of cour— Yes, my lord." Annabelle realized she was treading on very thin ice.

"Hmm." Richard found it difficult to accept some female's opinion. But after all it was, as she said, more of a "housekeeping matter." "Very well," he finally agreed. "You may take whatever can be cleaned off the replacement list. Now we must continue. . . ." He turned and strode to the next room.

As the hour passed, Annabelle was surprised they managed to rub along reasonably well. However, despite his invitation to make suggestions, she found his acceptance became decidedly testier the more ideas she offered.

"This fireplace and hearth shall have to be torn out and rebuilt."

Annabelle looked at the lovely hand-painted Florentine tiles of the decorative facing in alarm. "Oh surely, sir, you can save—"

"Annabelle." The earl had reached his limit and cut her off. "You will kindly allow that I know more about construction than you. The structure of this hearth is obviously unsound."

"Of course, my lord," Annabelle assented and carefully wrote that the fireplace was to be removed.

Satisfied that she had obeyed, the lord turned to consider the rest of the chamber. Once his attention was distracted, Annabelle added to the notation that the fireplace tiles were to be removed before tearing out the structure, and replaced on the new fireplace. She smiled in satisfaction. There was no sense in allowing the destruction of something so lovely just to let him show he knew more than she did.

Having discovered that little subterfuge, Annabelle often found herself merely adding additions to his instructions, making small changes and including necessary items on her own. After all, with all of these pages and pages of notes, it wasn't likely he would ever remember exactly what he had and hadn't said. It was much simpler to add what she wished than to argue with him over every little detail.

It was well into the noon hour as they finally finished the east wing. "We will quit for now," Richard advised her as they made their way back to the central rooms. "Mrs. Gavin should have a luncheon prepared. We have gotten considerably more accomplished than I had expected. I believe we should finish by early afternoon, that is, if you are not too tired to continue on."

"Oh, no. Of course not." Annabelle forced a smile. She wasn't sure which ached worse, her head or her feet. But perhaps with an hour's rest she would recover. By now she had firmly determined that she could never leave the castle's repairs to his discretion. Heaven only knew what treasures he would destroy or cast out.

Richard considered the girl a moment with approval. He knew she must be extremely tired, as he himself was, but she was obviously determined to make up for her previous lamentable behavior. He could scarcely fault that. "You must take some time to rest. Meet me back in the library at two o'clock." He reached out a hand for the lists she had been writing.

Annabelle clutched them closer to her suddenly concerned about her unauthorized additions. At his look she quickly came up with an excuse. "With your permission, sir, I'd like to rewrite these more neatly once we have finished. I truly fear, as I was writing so fast, my hand is next to illegible. I doubtless have made horrid spelling errors."

"Very well." The earl nodded with an inward smile. The girl was almost too eager to please him. As he had thought, all it had taken was a bit of firm direction. "I would like to have the completed lists on the morrow."

"Yes, my lord," Annabelle demurely agreed. The earl

was proving easier to handle than she'd expected. In the rewriting, it shouldn't be overly difficult to further conceal her own addenda to his notes. Also by the morning, he would be even less likely to recall his exact instructions.

She was almost looking forward to the afternoon. It would be quite interesting to renovate the castle. There were several more things that she would like done in the nursery wing, she mused on the way to her room. That dark paneling definitely would never do. The earl had begrudgingly allowed that it could be painted, but—she wrinkled her nose. No. Paper perhaps? That was it! Something like the Oriental Bird pattern she'd glimpsed that time when Lord Dunne took her and her mother to the Prince's pavilion in Brighton. After all, the earl had made it quite plain that he had no intentions of living in the castle. He was merely putting it in order for the children, and to preserve his inheritance. So, she thought, why should it not be decorated to please those who would be living there? But just how was she going to manage to have a particular wall covering ordered?

The afternoon found them in the oldest section of the castle. Annabelle loved the magnificent North Sea wing of the castle, which hung cantilevered over the cliff it was built into. The section was the original castle keep, and had rooms of wonderful proportions, with long gracious windows and breathtaking views of the ocean below. Unfortunately, it had remained unused over several generations. The fierce, cold salt winds had succeeded where long-past sieges by enemies had failed. Boarded windows had been breached by the relentless battering of the sea winds. The once-majestic gallery overlooking the expanse of water was now a haven for the gulls that rose in screaming protests from their nests on massive carved mantels and cornices when they entered.

"Good God!" Richard looked in disgust at his boots where he had unwittingly stepped in the years of gull droppings and discarded grey feathers. "Do not come in here, Annabelle, you will ruin your slippers—" He glanced down and was startled to find the girl was also wearing a man's—or boy's—sturdy footwear.

Annabelle was holding her skirts up away from the mess and so had revealed her secret. "Oh, my." She blushed. "I wore a pair of Terry's old boots as I feared the floors would be quite spoiled in this wing."

Richard drew his thoughts from the unwanted image of the delicate feet that would fit into an eight-year-old child's boots. "Have you no boots of your own?"

"Well, no. But Terry has outgrown these, so it's quite all right."

The earl's jaw tightened in anger at the penury his father's steward had imposed on this family, but he made no comment, determining to right the matter as soon as possible. "You knew the state of this wing? Surely Pitwick has not allowed you and the children to be roaming about here? It is obviously unsafe."

"No, my lord," Annabelle reassured him. "Actually, I do not believe Alvin even had keys to this section." Which was the real reason she had never managed to get in, but she didn't mention that fact. "We often walk on the beach below, and we could see that many windows were opened to the elements."

Richard grimaced. "What little I now know of the twins, I am surprised they did not decide to scale the cliffside to explore the wing on their very own."

"It was too steep." At his sharp look, she amended, "For me to allow the twins to even play near it, of course." Annabelle smiled reassuringly. Alvin would certainly never mention the embarrassing episode when he'd had to retrieve Lizzie and her from that very ledge. As the earl turned away, she subconsciously rubbed the elbow that yet held a scar from that near disaster. But they had known this wing must be marvelous. And it was! Disregarding the earl's instructions, she cautiously followed him into the chamber.

"I fear this entire wing is likely to be beyond salvaging," Richard remarked, to Annabelle's horror.

All this gothic grandeur overhanging the ocean to be abandoned! She glared at the back of his head, before raising her eyes up in wonder at the carved spiral colonnade that held up the graceful high arches of the ceiling. She would not let him leave this to further damage from the elements. But Annabelle already knew from her short experience that she had to come up with an excellent reason. For an undertaking this massive, he would likely have to think it was his own plan.

Innocent of his companion's plotting, Richard proceeded across to the next chamber, having forgotten in his disgust at the ravagement that he had bade her to stay back. "Come, I shall just check a few of these apartments to ascertain whether there is anything salvable."

Annabelle mentally ran through what little she knew of the man. What would convince him? Obviously, from the cavalier manner in which he had reeled off previous improvements with no apparent thought to cost, he had sufficient wealth for the undertaking. Typically, the servants had informed her of that steward's perfidy. But Alvin had also mentioned that the earl had brushed it off as of no great matter, advising him that he had his own fortune from numerous shipping concerns. Ah—Annabelle smiled—that was it! He was doubtless proud of having made his own way without aid from the family coffers. He loved the sea. And, whether he admitted it or not, she had become aware that he did hold a certain pride in this ancient country seat of the earldom.

"I believe I have seen enough—" Richard began after but a brief glance into the equally grim adjoining room, but Annabelle quickly cut in before he could finish the condemning statement. It would be much more difficult to make him go back against his own stated opinion.

"Oh dear, what a pity it would be if you could not see your way to reopening this magnificent wing. I recall Alvin mentioning that this was the original keep of the first castle."

"Why yes, that is true." Richard gave it another disparaging glance. "But I fear—"

"I suppose it is unavoidable, considering the monies involved." Annabelle interrupted again with a glance of sympathetic understanding that, as she expected, caused those fierce brows to draw together in annoyance. "That is, we are all of course aware of how your steward, that dreadful Mr. Hobbs, apparently managed to bleed the estate all of these years without you even suspecting." She noted with satisfaction the thunderous look creeping into the earl's eyes.

"Hobbs was my father's steward," Richard fairly growled, outraged that the girl dared intimate that he could have been so gullible. "I had nothing to do with the running of this estate until my ship docked less than a week ago."

"Of course, my lord! I did not mean to imply—" she stammered in apparent innocent confusion. "I—I was merely thinking what bringing all of this back to its original grandeur would cost, and of course, with the rest of the castle—" She hesitated, and then as if having a terrible thought, looked up at him in horror. "Oh, sir! I do hope it is not, that is, I can well understand what a frightening expense it can be to raise children, and of course, discovering you have the responsibility of an additional five! I could not bear to think that we are the cause of you being forced to abandon this historic part of your birthright!"

She almost felt guilty as, to her surprise, the lord's growing anger turned swiftly to concern. Richard gently cupped her chin, forcing her to look at him. "My dear child, I will not have any of you considering yourselves burdens. My argument on reopening this wing has nothing to do with finances. It was merely a question of the practicality of rebuilding it all."

Annabelle found herself speechless. She had never had a man, at least one who wasn't a relative, touch her like that. And he was being so frighteningly kind. She shielded her thoughts beneath lowered lashes, sighing in disappointment as he removed his hand.

"Now, you mustn't concern yourself further." The earl smiled in amusement at the girl's sigh. Apparently, she felt he was just trying to appease her. "Whatever amount Hobbs managed to abscond with could not have made any real inroads into the estate, as the principal was well beyond his reach. But even were that not the case, my own fortune could easily cover the needs of all of you and the others without the least strain. I don't wish you to worry about any cost again, do you understand?" he firmly reassured her.

Annabelle could not force herself to meet his eyes. Did the man have to be this considerate? But her small bit of perfidy was for his own good. He would thank her one day for not letting him allow this wonderful wing to deteriorate further. She firmly drew her mind back to its purpose, and resumed her act. "Thank you, sir." She smiled tremulously, but allowed herself a long regretful glance about the room that he could scarcely miss.

"As a matter of fact, you have brought out a good point. This wing is quite historic. I suppose at the very least I should not allow it to fall into further disrepair."

"I believe you will be pleased that you did not, sir." Annabelle fairly smelled victory. "As I can only imagine this would surely be your favorite wing—with your love of the sea. That is, of course, if you ever did decide to reside at the castle for any time," she carefully added. "I should think you would wish these very rooms to be your private apartments. Can you imagine"—she led him confidently back into the main gallery of the mural hall—"having your library here with all of these wonderful windows providing a view overlooking the sea?"

The earl gave her an incredulous glance as she described the gaping glassless arches as "wonderful." However, as she so enthusiastically continued, he could not help but begin to see the room through her eyes.

"Those walls will have to be removed." She gestured to the rotted wood paneling of the rear three walls. "They could easily be replaced with bookcases, glassed cabinets, all of teak, of course. You could have a fine working area with your desk at this end before that fireplace." She weighed the room's massive twin fireplaces at either end. "And near the other fireplace there might be settees for a pleasant reading area."

She glanced at the earl to judge his involvement in her plan and was pleased to see him considering the room with new interest. "It seems it would be quite convenient to have your sleeping quarters in the large apartment we were just in, modernized of course. I believe at one time there was even a stairway from there down to the old ship harbor. I don't suppose that could be rebuilt—''

Richard came over to study the outer wall with sudden interest. ''I shouldn't think it an insurmountable problem. I had not even considered the walled harbor. My father once kept his yacht there when we were but children. As there doesn't appear much silting present, I'd think its channel and basin would have retained sufficient depth, even at low tide.''

''Depth, sir?'' The man had gone even beyond Annabelle's imaginings.

''For the *Southwind*,'' he impatiently advised. ''Take a note. . . .''

Which Annabelle happily did, though her fingers ached before the daylight was gone. The earl did such a thorough job of listing renovations for the whole wing before he was finished, that Annie could scarcely think of any improvements of her own to add on top of his desires.

CHAPTER SEVEN

"This whole situation is bloody impossible!" The earl slammed down the sheaves of paper just delivered by Annabelle for his inspection before even looking at them.

Alvin gave a startled jump at his lord's ire. "Milord, I am truly sorry but—"

"You come to me with only five more servants from the entire countryside? And only one of them a man capable for outside work? I recall telling you the estate will require literally dozens—immediately!"

The old man wrung his hands in agitation. "Milord, if you would but allow me a moment to explain. We are just coming into the spring planting. There is such a terribly short season in this clime that all family members, except the very youngest children, must help to get seeding done in time. Not to mention that our only close village, Branburg, has sadly declined since the castle closed. With so few jobs in the offing, many families have been forced to move nearer the cities."

The earl sighed, forcing himself to face up to the obvious. "It is not at all your fault, Pitwick. Please, forgive my temper. I fear this entire situation has been rather much on me. I suppose I will have to staff this place from London. At least I still have some contacts there who might give advice." He fell silent for a moment.

The old man quietly waited for him to continue.

"Apparently, this is going to be a much longer undertaking than I had hoped. I shall remove the children to London until the castle is, at least, in more reasonable order. Naturally, Mrs. Gavin will have to accompany us to serve as chaperone for Annabelle. However, if you would be so good, I would appreciate your remaining here to oversee the general household."

"Of course, Your Lordship," Alvin answered, dubious about how the earl planned to manage all those children in London.

"I shall be sending craftsmen and workers for the repairs of the structure as well as further household staff from London. I hope to be able to employ a good steward to send with them for direction. In either case, I shall myself be returning at intervals to determine the progress toward my ends."

"Of course, milord."

His decision made, the earl saw no reason to delay putting the plan into action. "You will advise Mrs. Gavin of these matters and have her bring all of the children to me in the library so that I may inform them that we are to depart immediately."

"To London!" The children were all quite excited about the change. These particular children were even more inclined to foresee the move as a grand adventure, due to their being raised rather unconventionally, quite outside Society's usual strictures. This was a situation that would have given His Lordship serious pause had he considered it.

"Sir, six small children are quite a lot to move at once into an unprepared household. Perhaps you should precede us and have arrangements in order—"

Having had little previous exposure to children, Richard waved aside Annabelle's startled attempt at reason. "Annabelle, you needn't be concerned. I shall, of course, employ sufficient nursemaids and nannies to relieve you and Mrs. Gavin of the responsibility for full care of the children once we have arrived," the earl blithely advised her. "As I will be traveling with you, I shall be on hand in case of any unexpected emergencies."

"But, we could hardly—"

"Now, I am sure you have much to do as I would prefer to have an early start in the morn."

"Tomorrow, Yer Lordship?" Mrs. Gavin gasped in astonishment as it was by then well past the noon hour.

"Yes. Tomorrow." Richard would not be deterred. "I have already told Ben to depart for the village to hire extra carriages for the journey." He gave the older children's attire an assessing glance. "As it would appear that there is considerable need of new clothing, you should only pack enough to suffice until the necessities might be purchased in London."

Mrs. Gavin frantically tugged on Annabelle's sleeve, but Annabelle dared risk no further attempt at reason, speaking instead of the other matter that concerned her.

"My lord, were the notes on repairs I delivered to you sufficient?"

"Notes?" Actually, Richard had never taken the time to read over them, but didn't care to admit to such oversight. "Oh, yes. The notes. They were excellent. I do appreciate your help."

"You are welcome." Annabelle smiled in relief that he hadn't noticed her addenda. "Now with your leave, sir, we will excuse ourselves as there is much to do if we are to depart on the morrow."

At the earl's perfunctory nod, Annabelle and Mrs. Gavin herded the children from the room.

"Heavens, child," the housekeeper began in distress as soon as the door closed, "couldn't you have tried to reason with the earl? I cannot believe he plans to just up and take all these children to London with so very little preparation!"

"We want to go to London!" the twins began to protest, but Annabelle quieted them.

"And so you shall." She gave them a stern look. "But you—all of you—shall have to be on your very best behavior."

"We always behave well!" Terrance indignantly declared, notwithstanding the fact that he had, not a half hour before, totally disrupted the morning lessons with a particularly fat toad he had captured and brought in from the garden.

Annabelle frowned repressively at him, but hadn't time for any further counsel. "You must come with me to your rooms so we may determine what you need to take to London."

One had to give credit to the earl for his organizational prowess, as indeed that evening three traveling coaches arrived at the castle. Richard also somehow managed to hire two women from the village to help with the packing and other preparations for the journey.

It was mid-morning before the carriages finally rumbled from the courtyard.

Annabelle and Mrs. Gavin each rode in a coach with

three of the children. Annabelle assigned the two youngest to Mrs. Gavin's coach, along with Elizabeth to help her, while she took charge of the more rambunctious twins and Cathy.

Kitty and a newly hired lad from the village rode in the baggage coach. Richard's own coach followed, but he chose to ride his stallion along with the two armed outriders he had managed to hire briefly away from their farming for the journey.

Watching Richard, Annabelle longed to be riding beside him. She wasn't looking forward to the long days of traveling closed up with the twins.

Happily the trip, though arduous, was managed without any untoward incident. Annabelle stifled a sense of unease as they slowed before the immense but very quiet Rothbury House. Being the last of the patrician mansions, it was a haunting example of Jacobean grandeur.

Once the carriages pulled to a stop, the earl leapt from his horse and strode up to the door. "Where in thunder are all the servants?" Richard muttered to no one in particular as he impatiently rattled the knocker a third time.

"They didn't know we were coming," Annabelle reminded him a bit curtly as she tried to keep the miraculously rejuvenated twins in tow.

Her reminder was met with little welcome. Richard merely gave her a cool look before slamming the knocker yet again.

"I'm coming—I'm coming," an annoyed voice called from somewhere in the interior of the mansion. Shortly, the door was flung open by a harassed housekeeper. Her look immediately changed upon seeing the earl. "Your Lordship! I am so sorry, milord. Come in—come in. I was clear back in the pantry when I heard the knocker."

Richard impatiently brushed past the woman, gesturing Annabelle and the children to follow. "Mrs. Cummings, is it not?" He had met the London housekeeper on his first brief visit. The woman offered a rather befuddled nod as she watched the seemingly endless stream of children appear.

"Where is the rest of the staff?"

"But—milord, Mr. Hobbs told the others they were to go. He said only I was to stay this week to close up Rothbury House on your orders."

"What?" Richard restrained himself with effort, aware of the milling children gathering around in interest.

"Those were not my orders," the earl finally managed evenly, realizing he had come upon yet another of Hobbs's perfidies. Doubtless, the scoundrel had determined the household accounts could be put to better use lining his own pockets. "Would you know where I might find these other servants?"

"I expect, milord, you might send to the Berkham Domestic Service, as that's where most of us were taken on from," the woman cautiously advised.

The earl made an exasperated sound. "I will ride down there myself before the place closes for the day." He turned to Mrs. Gavin. "I apologize for this unfortunate state of affairs, but perhaps the two of you can manage until I can get this matter settled."

"Yes, milord," Mrs. Gavin reluctantly agreed, as she was quite weary from the long journey.

Once the earl departed, the housekeeper turned to Annabelle and questioned, "Miss—?"

"Miss Annabelle is the earl's sister, Mrs. Cummings." Mrs. Gavin realized the earl had made no introductions to the dazed woman, and briefly introduced all the children.

"We had thought the late earl had only two children—Master John and Miss Cecelia," Mrs. Cummings couldn't restrain herself from exclaiming in some dismay.

"Lord Dunne was previously married twice—to Ladies Matilda and Elsbeth," Mrs. Gavin briefly explained. "I am sorry to have come on you like this, however we must get these children settled, and I fear the earl did not stop the carriages for a noon meal."

At the other housekeeper's look of panic, Annabelle sighed tiredly. "If you will be so good as to direct me to the nurseries, I will attempt to get the children settled. Perhaps the two of you can see to a luncheon?"

"But milady, there is little in the way of food in the house as—"

"Mrs. Gavin, why don't you send Kitty to the market with one of the drivers?" Annabelle broke in, realizing the enormity of the situation had apparently rendered both women incapable of decision-making.

"That would be a help, Mrs. Gavin," the housekeeper said hopefully, looking at the other woman.

"It's Dorothy—most call me Dot," Mrs. Gavin allowed to the other woman.

"And I am Mary," the other housekeeper responded in relief at the woman's friendliness.

"The nurseries," Annabelle prompted.

"Oh, yes, of course. This way, milady.

"I'm afraid the rooms haven't been used," the housekeeper hesitantly warned as she opened the upstairs doors.

"That is quite all right. I shall manage." Annabelle stoically dismissed the woman, allowing her to return downstairs and begin lunch, as she knew without food the children would quickly become irritable. It had been many hours since their breakfast.

The large room in which Mrs. Cummings left them, though obviously not recently used, was pleasing and bright, with long windows. Holland covers were over most of the furnishings, but Annabelle could make out the school tables at one end and the children's dining and play areas at the other. The fireplace was empty, and though it was spring, the stone building was quite cool and damp.

"Here, children," Annabelle said using her tactic of turning work into play, "let's see who can get their portion of the room uncovered first!" She divided the younger children into two teams, strategically putting one twin on each side. "Now, you must carefully fold the covers and stack them here."

She and Elizabeth directed the male servants to place the luggage they brought up in the two children's bedrooms opening off the nursery. Annabelle determined to sleep in the nanny's room adjoining the children's for the time being, so she would be nearby should any of them become frightened in the strange home.

"Oh, Ben." Annabelle stopped the coachman as he turned to leave after delivering a trunk. "Would you mind sending one of the boys up with some additional coal for the fireplace?"

In scarcely any time, Annabelle had a cheery fire burning in the grate. The children had uncovered all the furniture, and had the main nursery in reasonably neat order by the time the two housekeepers brought up trays laden with a quickly concocted luncheon of soup and sandwiches.

CHAPTER EIGHT

As the children had their lunch, Annabelle managed to get the bedrooms in order. Much as Annabelle had planned, after straightening up and finishing their meal, the children were quite content to lie down for an afternoon nap.

Once she had the children quiet, Annabelle went down to the kitchen in search of the housekeepers. She had feared the conflicting authorities would cause dissention. She was pleased to find them working quite companionably together preparing the more elaborate evening repast.

"Miss Annabelle, you shouldn't be down here," Mrs. Cummings said in horror as Annie casually went to pour for herself from the kitchen teapot. "I'll bring tea for you into the parlor."

Annabelle waved her away. "You are both much too busy to abide by conventions just now. And, to be honest, I am too tired to bother. Has anyone heard from Lord Dunne?" she asked as she sat at the wooden kitchen table.

"Oh, my heavens! I've totally forgotten!" Mrs. Gavin exclaimed. "The earl returned some time ago and asked that I have you meet with him in his library."

"Now?" Annabelle groaned. She had hoped to have a few minutes to rest while the children were sleeping.

"I expect you'd best. It has been quite over an hour ago since he made the request. I am sorry that I forgot. Here, dear"—she scooped up Annabelle's cup and tea—"now you run on along, and I'll fix a tea tray for the both of you."

Annabelle hesitated in the hallway outside Richard's library to glance in the mirror. She patted at her hair and smoothed her skirts to little avail before tentatively knocking on the door.

"Come in." Richard glanced up and his brows lowered in disapproval on seeing her.

"You wished to speak to me, my lord?"

"Yes. Some time ago, actually. I was beginning to think perhaps I should have come up to your sitting room," he quipped sarcastically, being himself tired and out of patience with the state of affairs.

Annabelle didn't wish to cause Mrs. Gavin trouble and merely raised her chin determinedly, making no comment.

This had the unfortunate effect of aggravating Richard all the more. "Was the nursery area sufficient for the children?" the earl coolly inquired.

"Yes, sir. It is quite sufficient. The children are at the moment taking their naps."

"I gather Mrs. Gavin and Kitty managed well enough for today, then," he commented, much to Annabelle's annoyance as she had had little help in the matter. "I have reemployed the old staff plus extra servants, and will begin interviewing for a competent governess for the children immediately."

Annabelle gave him a somewhat startled look—a sea captain who knew nothing about children planned to employ their governess? "I would be pleased to offer my assistance on the selection of a governess, my lord, as I have had considerable experience—" she carefully began, but Richard coldly cut her off.

"I am quite capable of selecting a teacher for the children, Miss Ashley. The only matter I do require your assistance on is the renewal of their clothing, which is the matter I wished to speak to you about. I have prepared letters of credit for the various shops. The employment agency is also sending a seamstress out, but I expect you shall need to purchase whatever is required for immediate wear as well as what is impractical to make at home. If it meets with your approval, I will have a carriage at your disposal tomorrow."

Richard, a truly generous man, quite inadvertently failed to specifically mention that he intended Annabelle to see to her own clothing needs as well. She took his omission as deliberate.

"Of course." Annabelle tried to keep the sudden hurt from her voice. Obviously she, and perhaps even Elizabeth, were not "family" in his eyes. Annabelle could not meet his gaze. "Will there be anything else, my lord?"

Richard was disconcerted at the strange stillness in her face, as her temper usually matched his own, but before he could comment, Mrs. Gavin scratched at the door.

"I brought up a tea tray, milord, as I thought you could use a bit of refreshment. I know Miss Annabelle hasn't stopped all day for even a bite," the housekeeper blithely explained as she arranged the tray on a side table. "I do apologize for not telling her sooner that you wished to see her, but I fear Mrs. Cummings and myself have been so busy with the evening meal that we haven't even gotten upstairs, and with Kitty's been gone most the morning at the market . . ." Without awaiting a comment, she began pouring the two cups.

"I'm sure Lord Dunne would prefer his tea alone,"

Annabelle said quietly as she replaced the cup Mrs. Gavin handed her back on the tray. "If I may be excused, my lord?" Annabelle turned to leave, but Richard stopped her.

"No, you may not," Richard said tiredly, realizing how in the wrong he had been. "Please, sit down, Annabelle. That will be all, Mrs. Gavin."

Annabelle stiffly sat back down. The housekeeper worriedly looked at the two of them, but had little choice but to bob a brief curtsy and leave them to themselves.

"Why did you not tell me Mrs. Gavin hadn't informed you of my summons?"

"You didn't ask, my lord."

Richard sighed, asking himself why women were such blamed touchy creatures. "I assume from Mrs. Gavin's comments that you have been working all afternoon preparing the nursery and bedrooms?"

"Yes, my lord." Annabelle refused to look at him.

"For the love of heaven, Annabelle, would you stop this 'my lording' and look at me?" He ran a hand distractedly through his hair. "I realize I was wrong and apologize. It has been a very tiring and aggravating day. I return home to find that my father's bloody steward has released the staff and run off with all the funds for this establishment as well as my estate, and I have a house full of children with the place mostly under Holland covers—"

At that point Annabelle finally met his eyes.

Richard glared at her. "I simply will not be responsible for my actions if you say what you are thinking!"

Annabelle could not restrain the smile that tugged at the corners of her mouth.

Richard sheepishly grinned. "May I presume I am

forgiven enough to be allowed one of those scones on the tray?"

"Gladly, my lord." Annabelle innocently passed him the plate of pastries. "They are Mrs. Gavin's best, I believe."

Richard stopped with the pastry halfway to his mouth and surveyed it in dismay. "Mrs. Gavin's, do you say?"

"Oh yes, my lord."

Richard set the pastry back onto his saucer. "My name is Richard. It is not necessary that you use my title or constantly address me as 'my lord' when we are at home, Annabelle. We are, after all, family."

Annabelle carefully avoided his eyes. "Thank you, Richard. But as you know, Elizabeth and I are of no true blood kin to you—"

The earl waved his hand dismissively. "I consider you and Elizabeth as much my sisters as Cecelia and—"

"Catherine," Annabelle supplied.

"Oh yes, Cathy, of course. How could I forget her after that attack to my knee on our first meeting?" He chuckled. "She is the spicy little mite that looks so much like you."

Annabelle laughed. "We both take after my mother in looks."

"And temperament, no doubt," Richard dryly added.

"I am afraid I have been the one in charge of your new family for too long to easily allow someone else to take over," she cautiously allowed.

"Hmm." Richard considered her a moment. "You being left in charge of all the children was a most lamentable state of affairs caused, I admit, by my father's neglect. You must understand, it is a state which I intend ratifying. You are much too young for such responsibility."

"Sir, I must remind you I am nineteen—an age at which most young women are wed and with children of their very own," Annabelle sharply reminded him.

Richard gave her a patronizing smile. "You are, of course, quite correct. However, they do have husbands to help and advise them. Rather than having the onerous duty of tending to your siblings, you should be enjoying yourself at balls and routs, in order to find a husband and have those children of your very own."

"I do not consider the care and needs of my brothers and sisters an onerous duty, nor do I consider that I need some male to advise me!"

Richard laughed. "I am glad to see that you have regained a measure of your spirit. You worried me earlier. But, I am much too tired for a contest of wills at the moment. You must trust me. Purchase some pretty ball gowns tomorrow, and you shall discover how much more pleasing it is to dance the night away than remain at home as the resident nanny."

He hesitated a moment, before seriously adding, "However, as you are legally underage, I am your guardian as well as that of the younger children. I must advise you, I will not allow you to undermine my authority in the least."

CHAPTER NINE

The following morning Annabelle bravely prepared all the children for their shopping expedition with only Kitty to help, and the small entourage headed to Bond Street.

Word of the wealthy new earl had been spread through the *ton*, and his letters of credit were met by all shopkeepers with sequacious welcome.

Though they tried hard to pretend manly disinterest, even the boys enjoyed the purchasing of new outfits. By afternoon the extra carriage was fair bulging with packages and bandboxes.

Annabelle, though thoroughly annoyed at the earl's rather pompous attitude, found she quite enjoyed the novel experience of purchasing new gowns. In fact, due to that very attitude he had displayed, she purchased more than she might have otherwise. After all, if he wished her to be some "marriage mart" flirt, she saw no reason at all not to accommodate him.

At one last shop, Annabelle turned in front of the mirror to view herself in a particular ball gown. It was delightful, but dreadfully expensive. The pure silk skirt was layered over in white gauze sparkling with, it seemed, thousands of silver threads that were shot through it.

"Oh, Annie, you look like a fairy princess," Cecelia breathed softly.

"Thank you, love." Annabelle laughed. "I'm afraid really this is—"

"Ah, mademoiselle, you must take it. The dress is heavenly on you!" exclaimed the French modiste.

Annabelle looked at her image again longingly. "I do love it, but I fear the price is quite out of this world as well. I really don't think I should. I have already purchased quite enough."

"Oh, Annie. Don't be such a gudgeon," Terry impatiently piped up. "You know you want that dress. Besides, Richard won't mind the blunt. Just hurry so we might go home. I'm hungry."

"Terrance!" Annabelle said, sternly, correcting his manners. "You do not call Lord Dunne by his given name. Wherever do you come up with such terms as 'blunt'?"

"He said we could call him Richard." Thomas typically came quickly to his twin's defense. "The earl's our big brother," he importantly advised the interested sales staff. "He's buying me and Terry our very own mounts."

"Us, too!" Catherine glared at the boys.

"Well, yes, ponies perhaps," Terry disdainfully allowed.

"Annabelle and I are the only ones actually getting horses," Elizabeth coolly interceded. "All of you children are to have ponies."

"You are a child, too—"

"Oh, good heavens! Do behave yourselves—the lot of you!" Annabelle quickly stepped in to quell what she feared would soon be a roiling fight. "Whatever gave you the ridiculous notion that the earl was buying everyone mounts?"

"Why, he did, of course," Elizabeth advised her in surprise. "When we breakfasted with him only this morning. He insisted we must allow you to sleep late as you had worked so very hard. He said he was going to Tattersall's tomorrow. In fact, I think perhaps I shall go along—"

"You! If anyone goes it shall be us!" Terry fairly yelled. "No one takes girls to Tattersall's!"

"Children!" Annabelle began threateningly, but at the startled looks on the faces of the sales staff she forced a composed smile. "Kitty, would you mind escorting the children out to the carriage?"

"The dress, mademoiselle?"

So, the earl was quite intent upon taking complete charge of the children. Buying them all mounts, was he? Annabelle seethed. She would love to see him taking that lot for a ride in Regent's Park!

"Mademoiselle?"

Annabelle looked once again at her image and smiled. "Yes, I believe I shall take this one as well," she acquiesced. Letting her sleep late indeed! He had doubtless used the opportunity to bribe the children into his corner. "You may match it with slippers and gloves and send it on with the rest," Annabelle calmly instructed the delighted modiste. "You now well know my sizes."

"My lord, I would like to speak to you—" Annabelle began tersely.

"Later, my dear. I am afraid we were just now leaving."

Annabelle belatedly noticed the other man coming out of the library.

"Viscount Marquand." Richard introduced the man rather perfunctorily. "I would like to present my family."

Annabelle felt herself coloring as the lean young

dandy actually pressed his lips firmly to the back of her hand rather than the acceptable faux kiss.

"Charmed, Miss Ashley," he drawled, his fingers lingering on hers. "And where has this rogue brother of yours been hiding you all of this time?"

"I believe we are going to be late for our appointment, Marquand." Annabelle was relieved to have the earl firmly remove her hand from that of the other man.

The viscount merely winked surreptitiously at her before turning to him. "Of course, old boy. I shall look forward to seeing you again, my dear."

Richard reassuringly met Annabelle's startled glance and smiled. "I shall return in time for dinner and we may speak then."

Annabelle was somewhat amazed to find the town house functioning quite smoothly. Barton, the re-hired butler, had opened the door for them as though he'd never been gone a day. The remainder of Holland covers were nowhere in sight. All rooms smelled freshly of beeswax, and vases miraculously brimmed with cut flowers. Uniformed maids appeared as from nowhere to sweep the children and packages up to the nursery.

"Miss?" Barton discreetly took her cape and smoothly vanished with it, leaving Annabelle momentarily standing alone in the hallway.

"Ah, there you are, dear." Mrs. Gavin came up to her. "Mrs. Cummings is having one of the maids bring your tea. I told her to bring it to the rose parlor." She directed Annabelle to the nearby door. "As it seems to be cooling off considerably this afternoon, I've taken the liberty of having a cheery fire prepared for you."

"But Mrs. Gavin, I must go up and see to the children's tea. They were getting quite hungry."

The housekeeper laughed as she took Annabelle's reticule from her hands and set it aside, gesturing her into a comfortable armchair before the fire. "The maids are already on the way upstairs with the children's tea trays, and Lord Dunne managed to hire an absolutely delightful woman only this morning as nanny. It appeared a local family released her just this week when their last son left for Eton. She raised all five of their children, so she has had extensive experience. We were so very fortunate that the agency sent her to us first. I believe you will be pleased with her. Her name is Sarah Carstairs—"

"Mrs. Gavin!" Annabelle stopped that woman's happy rattlings. "We have only been gone for half a day's shopping, and I feel as though I have come back into a completely different household."

"Well, my dear, all it takes is a proper staff. And Lord Dunne, as you know, is quite generous. He said he absolutely refuses to have anyone overworked when there are so many people who need positions. The place is fair running with maids. Why, it will take both Mrs. Cummings and myself just to keep them all organized. Oh, here is Deidra with your tea now."

Annabelle bemusedly watched as a young woman she'd never seen before set the tray onto the tea table with smooth efficiency.

"Will that be all, miss?"

"Yes. Thank you."

The smiling maid bobbed a curtsy and left, discreetly closing the door behind her.

"Well, now isn't she the pleasant one? Lord Dunne apparently has quite the knack for procuring good people. Of course, I suppose as they say, you get what you pay for." Mrs. Gavin contentedly poured Annabelle's tea. "Would you believe the dear man has raised all of our wages?"

"Oh, do sit down and quit fussing over me." Annabelle felt as though she were suddenly suffocating from all the solicitude.

"Now, my dear, you must learn to take your proper place in society. I am so pleased that finally—"

"Oh, for heaven's sake, Mrs. Gavin, we have been having tea together for five years. Please do sit down. I feel as though my head is in a whirl from all of this." Annabelle distractedly rubbed her temples.

"Oh, have you a headache? I can ring for—"

"No, no." Annabelle irritably waved her back. "Please don't ring for another of the earl's miraculous staff!"

The housekeeper considered the girl a moment before chuckling softly. She finally relented and sat down, pouring herself a cup of the tea.

"That is much better." Annabelle apologetically smiled, picking up one of the pastries on the tray. "Why, this crumpet is simply excellent, Mrs. Gavin. Did you—?"

"Oh heavens, no." The housekeeper laughed. "You are well aware I have no hand at pastry. Why, even my own dear mother, God rest her soul, despaired of my ever learning to bake so much as a proper scone, and I fear Mrs. Cummings is almost as bad. The new cook, Mrs. Sutton, worked in France a bit, before all the current unpleasantness and"—at Annabelle's look she cut the story short—"well, suffice it to say, she is good with pastries. Now finally you shall no longer have to be doing the household baking."

Annabelle finished the crumpet with little pleasure. "It appears I shall no longer be needed for much of anything."

"Why, my dear child!" The housekeeper compassionately patted her hand. "You are feeling quite set aside are you not? I feared you might be. But now you'll do good to listen to me, and do listen well. You are a young lady and it is nigh time you were allowed to act as one. And there is certainly no one that deserves such good fortune more! Heaven only knows how Alvin and I have appreciated your good humor and help. I can't even think how we would have gotten by without it! What with your baking and washing the clothing, and teaching the little ones when, by all that's right, you should have been doing nothing more arduous than selecting pretty gowns from pattern books!"

Annabelle couldn't help but laugh at the vision. "Oh, come now. Can you truly imagine me with nothing to do all day but stare at some silly pattern book?"

The housekeeper laughed, too. "I expect you shall always find something to do. Which brings to mind, His Lordship said he has a gentleman coming by tomorrow he hopes will make a suitable steward to send out to the castle. He mentioned that he'd like you to be available for the discussions of what might be necessary regarding the decorating."

Annabelle brightened considerably. "Good. You will be sure to let me know the minute this gentleman arrives?"

Feeling much more optimistic, Annabelle soon headed up to the nursery to form her own opinion on the new nanny. No stranger, despite her experience, was likely to find handling those particular six children an easy task, she reassured herself. The poor woman was probably in desperate need of help by now.

She could not keep the unreasonable pique from her features on discovering the children all peacefully sleeping and the nursery in neat-as-a-pin order.

A plump, middle-aged woman came from the nanny's room and gave a nervous curtsy on seeing Annabelle's expression. "I am Sarah Carstairs, milady. Is there something amiss?" She anxiously glanced about the nursery to see what had caused such displeasure on the young woman's features.

"Amiss? Yes, this should be my place and it does seem to have gone amiss."

"Your place, miss?" Sarah looked at her in panic. Good heavens, had another nanny shown up for the position? The young woman's dress was rather an old style, but with that delicate beauty she would have never taken her for a servant! She had been so relieved when the agency had called her. At her age it was difficult to find a good job, and the earl had been so kind. But if this lovely young woman wanted the position, she wouldn't stand a chance! "Has His Lordship changed his mind about me?" she finally managed to ask.

"Changed his mind?" Annabelle sought to bring her thoughts back to order.

"You said this was your position. Does that mean—"

Annabelle looked at the worried woman and realized what she must be thinking. "Oh, heavens no. Mrs. Carstairs, is it? I am Annabelle Ashley, the children's older sister."

"Oh, Miss Ashley! I am so sorry. I didn't intend any affront!"

"Now, now, my dear woman." Annabelle caught the older woman's hands to stop their wringing. "There was no affront taken. I should have introduced myself. It is I who owe you an apology for causing you such concern."

"Not at all," the nanny assured her, even more flustered by Annabelle's actions. "I just feared—that is—if there is anything at all, milady, that you would like changed—?"

"Changed? It appears you have worked wonders. Here, come sit down. I'm afraid I must admit I had—I guess—hoped to find you had not managed quite so well."

"I do not understand, miss."

"Annabelle, please. May I call you Sarah?" At the other woman's bemused nod, Annabelle explained. "You see I have pretty much raised these children—well, Mrs. Gavin and I—"

It was not long into Annabelle's explanation that the older woman was smiling sympathetically. "Miss Annabelle, you do not have to explain to me how it feels to fear you are no longer needed! But you have no worries where these children are concerned. Why, they have been about nothing else but telling me of their Annie. And I assure you, I will doubtless need all the help and advice you can provide. The only reason I was able to get the mites down so easily today is that they were apparently quite worn out from your shopping! Why, those twins . . ."

The two women parted sometime later quite in charity with one another.

"I suppose I had better see if I can find where this army of maids has moved my belongings in time to dress for dinner!" Annabelle laughed as she took her leave from the nursery.

Happily, a chamber maid was just coming from a room down the hall and directed Annabelle to a nearby suite.

"His Lordship had us put you in these rooms, milady, as he expected you might wish to remain near the nursery. He said if these were not suitable, however, that we were to move you wherever you wished."

Annabelle glanced about in pleasure as she was led into the beautifully appointed rooms. "This will be quite fine."

"My name is Kerin, miss. Me, and Cassie here, are the upstairs chamber maids." She bobbed a pert curtsy. "I will be getting you more coal for your fireplace now. Would you be wishing a bath before dinner?"

"A bath would be heavenly!" Annie exclaimed, smiling at the girl's light Irish lilt.

"One of the men will be bringing the tub up then, miss. Shall I be sending your maid up to you?"

"I don't have a personal maid as yet—" Annabelle began, but the other girl gaily smiled a knowing smile.

"Oh, but of course you do. His Lordship, he hired Brit when he hired me this very morning. We are the both of us from Ireland, and had been working for Baron Smythson. Brit was Lady Smythson's lady's maid, and as they shall be moving back to the Continent, we applied here."

"My own lady's maid—what next?" After Kerin left to fetch Brit, Annabelle smiled to herself with kinder feeling toward the earl. Apparently, His Lordship had thought of everything.

CHAPTER TEN

"Good lord, man, Who is that Incomparable?"

"What?" Richard turned from where he was pouring his friend, the Duke of Heatherton, a brandy. He almost didn't recognize Annabelle. She stood speaking to Mrs. Cummings just outside the open door to the library. The deep rose dinner gown she wore was accented by silk rosebuds pinned in her raven locks. Her curls had been gathered up high at the side to cascade in splendid riots down her back.

"If you tell me that woman's your wife, I may well have to have you killed, my friend," the duke remarked sotto voce as Annabelle smilingly dismissed Mrs. Cummings.

The earl raised his brow. "My dear fellow, surely you know I am a confirmed bachelor!" Still, he couldn't help pausing to admire Annabelle for a moment before calling to her.

Annabelle turned to the library in surprise. "Oh, Richard, I didn't know you had returned home."

"Would you come in for a moment?"

Annabelle curiously glanced at the other quite elegant man as she entered.

"Charles, I would like to present my sister, Miss Annabelle Ashley. Annabelle, Charles Eddingfield, the Duke of Heatherton."

"Your Grace." Annabelle curtsied before the tall man.

With great difficulty the duke drew his eyes from the row of delicately embroidered rosebuds edging the neckline of her dress. "Your—sister?" He glanced at Richard. "I recall you having said your sister was but a lass in leading strings."

"Ah, one of them is—or two, rather. Actually, since I last spoke with you some weeks ago, I have—shall we say, discovered—that I have four sisters as well as three additional brothers."

The duke eloquently raised his brow. "I had heard that your father had previously married Lady Matilda, but I had not realized there were other children," he murmured, studying Annabelle for a moment. "But surely, you could not be—?"

Annabelle cleared his confusion. "My mother was also previously married to Lord Dunne."

"Ah. I see." Charles eyed Richard considering. "However, a sister is a sister, right, old man?" he finally decided. "You did say I was invited for dinner?"

"Of course," Richard dryly agreed as he walked over and pulled the tasseled cord to page Barton. "Annabelle is actually one of the reasons I wished to speak with you, Heatherton. As I have been rather out of touch with the *ton* of late, I had hoped you might know a likely patroness to procure vouchers to Almack's for her."

"I would be most delighted," the duke easily agreed. "Why, Lady Jersey, it happens, owes me a favor just now. As a matter of fact," he said, warmly smiling down at Annabelle, "since I am sure Lord Dunne is quite busy what with remodeling the castle and settling all these children, I shall escort you to Almack's myself, Miss Ashley."

"You in Almack's, Heatherton?" The earl laughed, giving Annabelle no chance to even comment. "I'm grateful, however, I fear I cannot allow that. Annabelle has not yet been presented to Society. I will escort her—as her guardian, of course."

"You will excuse me, gentlemen," Annabelle coolly spoke up, "but I don't seem to recall either of you so much as inquiring as to my interest in this Almack's."

Both men stared at her speechless as Barton came to the doorway and inquired, "You rang, milord?"

"Uh, yes. His Grace shall be staying for dinner, Barton."

As soon as Barton left, Richard rounded on Annabelle, but the duke forestalled him with a bark of laughter. "The deuce! I expect history might have been made here! An earl and a duke put down by a school miss in one sentence! We do owe you an apology, my dear." He glanced at Richard and grinned. "And, as your brother is still glowering, so I shall make it on his behalf as well."

"Thank you, Your Grace."

Richard made no comment, but his look bode ill for the future.

"Have you truly something against Almack's? It was my understanding that to appear in those 'hallowed halls' was every young woman's dream," the duke continued incredulously.

"To be truthful, I fear I know very little of the place. This is actually the first time I've been to London."

"Delightful! We shall be allowed to educate you," the duke facetiously announced, drawing her over to be seated at the couch. "Now, Almack's is an ignoble building of assembly rooms on King Street, composed of architecture most unremarkable. It is ill ventilated and generally quite overcrowded. The refreshments consist of watered-down lemonade, insipid ratafia, and stale sandwiches—"

By this time Annabelle, who was beginning to quite like the unpredictable man, found herself smiling. "Sir, I cannot believe you would so try to cozen me. If that were so, why would anyone wish to frequent it? I must admit though, that you have made me curious. What is this Almack's really?"

The duke drew himself up in pretended affront. "'Pon my oath, Miss Ashley thinks this but a Banbury tale. Dunne, you must vindicate me at once."

"I fear His Grace's description is quite to the point. If anything, he does it too much justice. However improbable, it is considered quite essential for young females to be presented there in order to meet an eligible *parti*." He looked at her consideringly. "I didn't realize you had never been to London. My father always opened the town house during the Season. I assumed all of you must have come with him."

"The late earl quite often brought my mother here, but he preferred we children remain at his estate at Swansea," Annabelle explained.

"Hmm." Richard decided to excuse her previous behavior, realizing she must know very little of the ways of the *ton*. "Well, I shall insist you rely on my judgement in these matters." He turned to the other man. "Heatherton, isn't your sister Victoria similar in age to Annabelle?"

"Why, yes." The duke immediately saw Richard's direction. "Vicky is, in fact, being presented this Season. As I have, myself, just returned from the Continent, I am not up to scratch on my mother's machinations, however, I am certain Vicky would be quite pleased to meet Miss Ashley. Perhaps they might drop by tomorrow on their morning calls?" He turned back to her.

Annabelle found herself blushing upon also reading Richard's intent. "Your Grace, we would certainly not wish to impose on your family—" she began in embarrassment, bringing an indignant glare from the earl.

The duke again quickly interceded to ward off the disaster brewing in his friend's eyes. "My dear child, your brother and I have been running together since our salad days. I would consider it quite a pleasure should our families manage to rub along. On that matter, although Lord Dunne insists he is a confirmed bachelor, I have been plotting to throw Vicky into his path."

Annabelle grinned at the look Richard gave his friend, but their banter was put on hold as Barton came in to announce dinner.

Despite the earl's very firm denouncement of any intent to seek a wife, Annabelle noted he made no attempt to excuse himself the following morning when the dowager duchess brought Victoria by to call.

Victoria was an incredibly lovely girl some two years younger than Annabelle. She had golden curls cut in the new *à la greque* short fashion with ringlets about her face, a pert, nose, and perfect Cupid's bow lips. And as far as Annabelle could tell, she had absolutely no trace of any serious intellect at all. Nonetheless, Annie couldn't help but like the girl, who had apparently inherited the same delightful friendly nature as the duke.

"Annabelle, I am just so glad Charles told us about you," Victoria confided happily as Annabelle poured tea. "Everyone has been all in a hum about the new Earl of Rothbury and his huge family." She cast an innocently alluring glance at Richard from under long lashes. "Charles mentioned you didn't even know you had seven brothers and sisters, my lord?"

"I have lived primarily in the West Indies for some time," Richard offered by way of explanation. Annabelle was surprised to find herself unreasonably galled by the warm smile he gave the girl. "Would you like to meet them?"

"Oh, may I?" Victoria excitedly asked.

"I can take you up to the school room," Annabelle offered, rising, but Richard forestalled her.

"There is no need." He walked over to the bellpull. "You must not interrupt your tea. I shall summon one of the servants to have Mrs. Carstairs bring the children down presently."

"My lord, really, I think I had best—" Annabelle spoke softly, hoping to dissuade what she feared was a very unwise decision, but the earl stopped her protest with a stern look.

"Your father was a Major Seymour Ashley you say, my child?" the duchess questioned. Annabelle turned, getting caught up in explaining the relationships of all the children while trying not to listen to the apparently gay conversation in which the earl and Vicky were engaged.

"Ah, here they are." Richard smiled, as shortly the children filed into the room under Mrs. Carstairs's worried eye. "Your Grace, Lady Victoria, first I would like to present Elizabeth, Catherine, and Cecelia, my sisters."

Annabelle found herself holding her breath as the girls, all hastily coached by Sarah, stepped forward and curtsied quite solemnly.

"And next, my brothers, John David, Terrance and Thomas," he continued. The boys bowed, though a bit awkwardly.

"Children, the Duchess of Heatherton and Lady Victoria."

"Why twins, yet!" the duchess exclaimed. "And so very identical. Richard, I don't see how you tell them apart."

"He can't," the first twin broke in.

"I'm Thomas, he's Terry," the second twin corrected the order. "But that's all right." He grinned at the earl. "Sometimes we can even fool Annie."

"Thank you," Richard dryly acknowledged.

"I chopped my foot!" John David decided the twins were getting too much attention and importantly stepped up to the duchess. "Would you like to see the—"

Elizabeth stepped hastily forward to stop him from stripping off his boot. "John David, the ladies do not wish to see any scars. Such things make them swoon."

"Really?" Terry asked with undue interest, which happily the earl noted and he moved over to clap a firm warning hand on the lad's shoulder.

"We would certainly not wish to make any ladies swoon just now, would we, boys?"

"But I never saw a lady swoon. Annie won't do stuff like that," Terry commented in disappointment. "All she did was yell when we put a toad down her—"

"Terrance, I am sure no one wishes to hear about that!" Annabelle quickly stopped him.

"Annie, I want my hair like that!" Cathy excitedly tugged at her skirt pointing happily to Victoria's curls. "Can you get that lady to fix it?"

"Dear, it's not proper to point." Annabelle apologetically smiled at Victoria. "And Lady Victoria does not fix hair. Mrs. Carstairs, perhaps you should—"

"Have you bwought my pony home, Wichard?" Cecelia lisped wrapping her arms quite around the leg of the startled earl, as she beguilingly looked up at him. "I want one with bwown spots!"

Annabelle and Victoria could not withhold the giggles that erupted on seeing the earl's face. Even the duchess suspiciously raised her handkerchief to her lips.

Mrs. Carstairs, much to her credit, managed to quite calmly extricate the earl from his predicament. "Come dear, I'm sure His Lordship will speak to you about the pony later."

"Yes," a red-faced Richard managed. "Thank you, Mrs. Carstairs. You may take the children back to the nursery now."

"But we haven't met the duke! I don't think we've ever seen a duke, have we, Terry?" Thomas complained as Mrs. Carstairs hustled them from the room.

"I must apologize to you ladies. The children have not had the opportunity to be in Society all that much," the earl said to the duchess, refusing to meet Annabelle's eyes.

"I won't hear a bit of it, Lord Dunne." The duchess smiled and added, "Actually, I find their naturalness quite refreshing. I could never countenance the idea that children are to be seen and not heard."

CHAPTER ELEVEN

"The Duke of Heatherton, my lord," Barton staidly announced, standing aside for the man to enter the parlor.

"Ah, Heatherton. Come in." Richard was privately glad his friend had not arrived some minutes earlier to witness his episode with the children, but then noticing Victoria's gleeful grin he had a sinking feeling the duke would doubtless hear all about it.

After having warmly greeted Annabelle, the duke turned to his family. "Mother. Vicky. I am pleased to find you have come by."

"I fear we must be leaving though," the duchess replied to her son. "We have quite a few other calls to make. It has been such a pleasure meeting you, my dear," she addressed Annabelle before turning to the earl. "We are attending the theater tomorrow evening and would be delighted if you and Annabelle would share our box."

Annabelle wryly watched as the earl, who had previously confessed to her a dislike for attending plays, readily accepted the invitation.

"I am so glad we met," Victoria exclaimed. "It shall be such fun being friends! We'll make other plans tomorrow evening."

Once the ladies left, Richard turned to Annabelle. "Heatherton and I planned to stop by Tattersall's to see if they might have some decent cattle at the auction. I shall also see about ponies for the children."

"You won't forget the brown spots?" she innocently inquired.

"How could I?" The earl chuckled without responding to the curious glance the duke gave him.

"Annabelle, this morning I have received a note that the Berkham Agency is sending out at least two governesses for interview at approximately one o'clock," he continued. "I expect I should be back before they arrive, but if not, perhaps you will tell Barton to have them await me in the library?"

"Of course. I would like the opportunity to speak with any applicants as well," Annabelle added, despite his earlier coldness when she had offered to help in the selection.

The earl's lips tightened. "I do not wish to discount your years of having to raise the younger children practically alone, however I think today in particular points out the need for a firmer hand in the future than I expect you would seek for them. I shall summon you when I have hired the governess," he announced.

After the men departed, Annabelle headed upstairs in exasperation. "Miss Annabelle." Sarah Carstairs came upon her. "I had wished to—" She hesitated on noting the girl's expression. "Why, is something wrong?"

"Oh, Sarah, how could that man be so pleasant one moment and arrogantly stubborn the next?" Annabelle sighed. "I am sorry," she began again on realizing the other woman had no idea of what she spoke. "It's Lord Dunne. He simply refuses to allow me to have any hand in the selection of a governess for the children. I really fail to see where a male who has spent the majority of his adult life aboard one sailing vessel or another, and has never even been around children, would have any notion of what to look for in a proper teacher."

"Well, I don't quite know what to advise you," Sarah logically answered, "but perhaps you might consider that His Lordship does seem to be quite intelligent and has really been most kind. I should expect he will make a good selection."

"I suppose. After all, he did select you." Annabelle finally smiled. "I guess I am worrying over nothing."

Nonetheless, Annabelle tried to remain close at hand to at least meet the applicants when they arrived. Unfortunately, Mrs. Cummings requested to speak to her about the week's menus. When she had finished with that, settled a minor dispute with a tradesman, and was free to return to the parlor, it was only to find the earl had already dismissed one applicant and was closeted with the second.

The first applicant, a pleasant-looking woman perhaps in her mid-thirties, was just replacing a worn woolen cloak about her shoulders as Barton stood by to usher her out.

"You have finished speaking with Lord Dunne so quickly?" Annabelle inquired, surprised as she had not been gone overlong.

"Yes, my lady." The woman quickly curtsied on finding herself unexpectedly addressed. "I do not believe His Lordship considered my credentials sufficient." The woman sighed in resignation with a disappointed glance at the neatly lettered sheets she had set on the hall table as she replaced her cloak.

"May I?" Annabelle picked up the sheets at the woman's surprised nod. "Mrs. West? You are recently widowed I see. I am sorry. Is this why you seek employment?''

''Thank you, my lady. Yes. I taught the village children for some years where we lived in Leicester. But I had to give up the post to remain with my husband when he became—'' She stopped and apologetically smiled. ''The village school, of course, had to replace me and can now only afford one teacher.''

''Have you children of your own?''

''No, my lady. We were never so blessed. I was raised in a large family and have always wanted children. I suppose that is one of the very reasons I enjoy teaching so. I taught at the Leicester school for ten wonderful years. They gave me an excellent reference.''

Annabelle realized she was unwarrantedly raising the woman's hopes and handed the sheets back to her in sympathy. ''I wish I had some word in the selection, Mrs. West, but I fear the decision is totally that of the earl.''

Annabelle impatiently paced about the parlor waiting to hear the library door open. Richard was certainly speaking a long time with the second applicant after having so summarily dismissed the kind Mrs. West.

Perhaps the other woman was even better, but Mrs. West had seemed to her to have excellent credentials. She heard the earl's voice and hastily sat down and picked up a magazine on hearing him inquire of her whereabouts from Barton.

''Annabelle,'' the earl addressed her upon entering, ''I would like to present Mrs. Thornton. Mrs. Thornton will be the new governess for the children. Miss Ashley is my step-sister.''

Annabelle only vaguely noted the addition of ''step''

into their relationship as she attempted to curtail her dismay at the appearance of the new governess.

There was nothing at all warm or soft about the rigid form of the older woman. Her dress, though dark grey and of a severe cut, was obviously of fine kerseymere sternly buttoned up to the chin with a long, neat row of expensive jet buttons, ending, Annabelle was surprised to note, with an enormous ruby pin. In fact, nothing of the woman's manner or outfit suggested any type of penury. But need, Annabelle tried to tell herself, surely should not be a factor in the selection of a teacher.

The tall austere woman nodded at the introduction. "Miss Ashley," she acknowledged in a firm, cultured voice.

"I am pleased to welcome you, Mrs. Thornton." Annabelle made a sincere effort to keep her voice friendly and not prejudge the woman. "I am sure you will enjoy teaching the children." She smiled. "Though they can be a bit rambunctious at times, you will find they all really have quite sweet natures."

"Children never remain 'rambunctious,' as you say, under my care for long, Miss Ashley, so you need have no concerns in that regard," the woman coolly advised.

Annabelle felt her temper begin to rise as she turned toward Richard.

"Perhaps you would like to meet the children now, Mrs. Thornton," Richard interceded with a warning look at Annabelle. "I shall ring for Mrs. Gavin to escort you. Annabelle, if I might have a word with you?"

"I fear you do not approve of my choice of governess," Richard began without preliminaries when they were alone.

"I was more polite to that woman than she to me,"

Annabelle snapped. "And you have quite made the point that my approval is unnecessary."

With difficulty the earl held his temper in check. "You must not expect Mrs. Thornton to kowtow to you, Annabelle. She is a noblewoman in her own right, though of impoverished circumstances that necessitate she seek her own way through teaching. I should not think you so small-minded as to hold her forced status against her."

Annabelle glared at him in fury. "Having resided for some years in rather impoverished circumstances myself, my lord, it is quite unlikely I should hold the woman's status against her, even if she is truly impoverished, which I doubt. That all but vulgar ruby she wore at her neck was quite a bit larger than your own signet stone."

She angrily gestured at the jewel-encrusted ring he wore.

Richard paused, then curtly said, "Probably paste, and even if it is not, the woman certainly has a right to have kept sentimental trinkets from happier days."

Annabelle made a rather unladylike sound suspiciously like a snort. "I would be most surprised if that woman even knew the meaning of 'sentimental' or 'happy'!"

"Miss Ashley—" the earl gritted out, and Annabelle realized she had again pushed him too far.

"Oh, Richard, I'm sorry. Maybe I am being unfair. I don't really know the woman. I just can't bear the thought of anyone treating the children harshly," she managed, looking down in embarrassment as her eyes treacherously filled with tears.

To Annabelle's surprise, the earl pulled her tenderly against him. "Listen to me, Annie. I assure you I will allow no one to harm the children. They are my brothers and sisters as well." The hand automatically stroking her hair in consolation hesitated, and Annabelle felt his long fingers seemingly become entangled in the thick curls. The earl became very still for a barely discernable moment before he set her firmly away from him. "Here now, dry those tears." He drew out a monogrammed handkerchief and handed it to her before casually moving away.

Annabelle felt her thoughts strangely unable to proceed beyond feeling the earl's arms holding her to him. She managed to dab at her eyes in silence to cover her confusion as he rather oddly considered her.

"Mrs. Thornton," he finally continued, "does have excellent credentials as well as references from several highly regarded families. She will be returning tomorrow to begin service. I must insist that you give her a fair opportunity to prove herself. After that, if you can come to me with any legitimate complaints, I shall reconsider my decision."

CHAPTER TWELVE

"Yes, Barton?" The earl glanced up from the morning paper as his butler came into the breakfast hall.

"A message has arrived for Miss Annabelle, my lord. I had thought she was down for breakfast."

"A message. From whom?" The earl sharply glanced at the silver tray which held a single white rosebud lying over a monogrammed envelope.

Annabelle at that moment entered the room. "Good morning, Richard. Did I hear someone mention my name?"

"One of His Grace's men delivered this a few moments ago for you, my lady." The butler smiled as he held out the tray.

"His Grace?" Annabelle picked up the rose in delight. "Oh, the Duke of Heatherton." She smiled on opening the note under Richard's watchful gaze. "Why, how very nice. He wishes me to go riding with him this morning in the park."

"Riding?" Richard picked up the monogrammed envelope, turning it over to expose the embossed ducal seal.

"Yes." She noticed the lord's frown. "Surely you have no objection as he is your friend?"

"Oh, no," the earl finally answered. "Heatherton is quite reputable."

Annabelle smiled happily, raising the rosebud to sniff its sweetness as she turned.

"Aren't you going to partake of breakfast?" the earl asked, stopping her.

"I had some tea earlier. I must hurry and change as he'll be here shortly," she called over her shoulder, lightly skipping from the room.

The earl found himself in an unaccountably bad humor when only a few minutes later Barton returned again to announce the arrival of Mr. Smythe.

"Smythe? Oh yes, the steward. Very well." Richard impatiently tossed the paper aside. "You may show him into the library."

Though of unprepossessing looks, Richard found the rather rotund young clerk apparently quite knowledgeable in the business end of running an estate.

"I have worked for the past five years as assistant to Lord Essex's steward," Robert Smythe explained. "Actually, I was in charge of the lord's Coventry estate and oversaw the renovation of his manor home there, so I feel myself well-qualified."

"I fear you will find my estate in Northumberland in considerably worse condition than Coventry's manor," the earl dourly quipped. He was, however, familiar with the Earl of Coventry and had a highly-worded written commendation of the young man's worth from him. "Very well. I shall, however, require that you immediately post to Northumberland. I have already employed a number of carpenters, stonemasons, craftsmen, and the like, but have delayed sending them up until I had a steward to escort them." He reached into a drawer. "Here we have a list of the necessary repairs and replacements—" He hesitated on recalling he had never checked the neatly printed pages after Annabelle had given them to him, but determined it was too late to worry about it then and handed them over. "You may wish to read over the pages to extract what supplies will be required. A great deal of the basic building materials can doubtless be obtained locally in Northumberland. You shall probably have to purchase the finer items here in London."

The steward glanced down the sheets with some concern. "My lord, there is of course no problem with the building materials and the like, but I notice there is also considerable notation on fabrics for draperies and the recovering of furnishings. Although you have had colors and pattern types listed, I fear that I really am not qualified to make the determinations on the exact style."

Richard picked up some of the sheets and smiled on finding notations such as "something mauvish would go well with the painted cornices—Peonies with hunter green leaves if we can find it."

"I do see what you mean." He reached for the bellpull.

"Barton, would you have Annabelle step in here for a moment as soon as she comes down?"

Annabelle stopped in some alarm on entering the room a few minutes later to find the two men so carefully studying her sheets.

"You wished to speak to me, sir?"

"Yes." Richard glanced up and hesitated for a long moment. The powder blue riding habit she wore was bordered by a darker blue braid trim that delightfully outlined the graceful female curves beneath.

"Is something wrong, my lord?" Annabelle anxiously inquired, realizing that Richard had likely discovered her additions in the papers.

"Wrong? No, I merely thought to seek your help yet

again." The earl drew his thoughts back to the matter at hand, and briefly introduced his new steward.

"Understandably, Mr. Smythe is not comfortable selecting fabrics and the like for Rothbury. As I see you have made considerable notes on color and patterns, I thought perhaps, if it is not too much trouble, I might impose upon you to make the actual selections?"

"Trouble? Why heavens no!" Annabelle exclaimed in delighted relief. "I would love to. In fact, I had hoped you might allow me to help."

Richard smiled at her enthusiasm. "Thank you. Harding Howell and Company, on Pall Mall, are one of the largest linendrapers. I shall have their clerks bring by samples for a start. There is no real hurry as the refurbishings can only be done once the place is thoroughly cleaned and the physical repairs made." He turned back to the steward. "Mr. Smythe, if you would take these sheets about to the local building suppliers and return with some costs?"

"His Grace, the Duke of Heatherton," Barton announced as the steward was taking leave.

The duke didn't even notice the somewhat less than warm greeting with which his boyhood friend met him as he lifted Annabelle's hand to his lips. "My dear, how absolutely charming you look today. I see you have even worn my rose."

Richard glanced up sharply to discover the white bud was indeed tucked into Annabelle's carefully styled curls. For some reason the sight rankled, an emotion he covered by politely escorting the pair out to where grooms awaited with the horses.

The duke had brought over a mount from his own stable for Annabelle. "Oh, she is beautiful, Your Grace!"

Annie stroked the small bay mare's sleek neck for a moment before the groom led her to a mounting block.

"You are welcome to continue to use the mare until the cattle Richard has arranged for arrive," the duke graciously offered, but Richard declined before Annabelle could answer.

"The mounts I procured for all the children should arrive at the stable on the morrow," the earl said, recalling with some pleasure the lovely almost blue-black Arabian on which he had outbid no other than Prinny's own stablemaster. Hopefully, the Prince Regent hadn't had his eye on that particular bit of blood for some special reason. But Richard hadn't been able to resist the odd vision that had taken his fancy of seeing Annabelle with her raven locks so near the same color riding the ebony beast.

Annabelle happily soaked up the warm sun and light, spring-scented breeze in silence for some minutes before noticing the duke's considering look. "Your Grace, you must forgive my manners. It is just so lovely out today, I fear I became completely enwrapped in it all," she apologized for ignoring him.

Charles laughed. "Not at all, Miss Ashley. I have quite enjoyed watching your pleasure. I am sure you must have been kept busy of late with having to completely reestablish the household here in London?"

"Establish, more than reestablish," she said laconically and grimaced. "But the earl has been kind and more than generous. I yet find it difficult to believe he has so readily accepted the situation. Can you but imagine suddenly finding you have a previously unbeknownst family of seven?"

"Heaven forbid!" The duke raised his brows. "Although as Mother is never wont to remind me, it is time that I established my own nursery. I cannot but admire Richard's fortitude on the advent of acquiring six siblings scarce more than babes! However, having you as the seventh doubtless would make the acquisition quite worthwhile." He smiled at Annabelle's rising color.

"Your Grace!" Annabelle protested in embarrassment. "I fear I have likely been more of a trial to Richard than the younger ones." She sighed guiltily, thinking of her indiscretions with the castle notes. She carefully chose to ignore the duke's inquiring glance. "Actually, Cecelia and John David are the only infants. They are respectively four and five years of age." She listed the children, their ages and relationships, and soon had the distinguished duke surprising himself as he laughed aloud at their peccadillos.

"A ghost?" The duke guffawed to the astonishment of nearby riders in St. James Park, as she told the tale of Melissa. "What I wouldn't give to have seen Dunne's face."

Annabelle giggled. "Oh, I should probably not have told you about that, Your Grace. Richard would have my hide if he only knew."

"It shall be our secret, my dear." The duke unremorsefully wiped away the tears caused by laughing so with this amazingly unaffected young woman.

"Charles, I insist you introduce me to such an entertaining companion."

Neither of the pair had even noticed the elegantly beautiful woman who, with her escort, had cantered up beside their ambling mounts.

"Ah, Countess." The duke smiled, pulling his horse to a halt. "Forgive me, this child has quite made me forget my surroundings. The Countess Lieven, Miss

Ashley." The duke performed the introductions. "Miss Ashley is the Earl of Rothbury's sister."

"I had heard that the new earl had taken up residence in town with a rather large family?" she queried politely. Annabelle was not unwilling to explain the situation to the surprisingly friendly countess.

"How absolutely droll!" the lady delightedly declared when she had finished. "So the earl knew nothing of his father's second marriage? I must hear more of this story. I am having a dinner Friday evening and shall have invitations sent over for you and your dear brother," she advised the rather surprised Annabelle. "I'm sure you've already received yours, Charles?" At the duke's acknowledgment, she continued, "It is refreshing to find new faces in the *ton*, Miss Ashley. Doubtless, the earl will bring you to Almack's Thursday?"

"Actually, I intended seeking out Lady Jersey for vouchers today," the duke said, "as both Miss Ashley and Dunne are newly in town."

"Lady Jersey? Heavens, Charles, why didn't you call upon me?" She flirtatiously tapped his arm with her riding crop. "I shall have vouchers sent over this evening, my child," she assured Annabelle before turning back to the duke. "I expect you've heard of course that Sophia Wellington has retaken residence at Blairstone Manor?"

Annabelle was surprised as the duke's friendly manner turned suddenly very cold. "No, I had not. Her husband accompanies her, no doubt?"

"Husband?" Countess Lieven raised her brow in surprise. "Charles, I thought surely you would have known. Percival succumbed nearly a year ago to the consumption with which he was plagued since childhood."

The duke stared at the countess dumbfounded. "Consumption? Sophia made no mention of the man suffering consumption. I—I had no idea."

"No? She doubtless would not have told anyone. Sophia always did have a ridiculous sense of loyalty."

"Loyalty!" he sniffed in disdain.

"I had contemplated inviting her to the dinner on Friday," the countess threw out, only to be firmly thwarted by the duke.

"In which case, I shall have to send my regrets, Countess. You will excuse us." With a look at Annabelle, he turned his horse and moved away.

Annabelle glanced in embarrassment at the other woman. The countess, however, appeared unmoved by the intentional cut and merely watched the man depart with a look of keen speculation. Seeing Annabelle's concern, the countess lightly smiled and gave a friendly nod before turning her own horse away.

Annabelle was somewhat appalled as no sooner than they were away from the countess, they were approached by a seeming endless group of other riders seeking introductions.

Apparently, being seen escorted by the Duke of Heatherton as well as receiving a public acknowledgment by the Countess Lieven was more than enough to encourage the London *ton* to satisfy their curiosity about her. By the time the duke had rather curtly dismissed his peers, Annabelle had been introduced to more titles, both male and female, than she realized existed.

"Well, Miss Ashley, you shall doubtless find an avalanche of invitations upon your hall table come the morrow," Charles rather formally advised her when at last they sufficiently extricated themselves from the crowds to continue their ride.

"I must admit I find the mere thought of so many unending balls and musicales and soirees a bit overwhelming," Annabelle said lightly, curious about his distracted manner.

The duke absently nodded. Annabelle was certain he hadn't the slightest idea what she'd said. She studied the hard, closed look on his face in worry. Finally she couldn't resist and hesitantly inquired, "Is this Sophia someone you cared for?"

The man turned on her with a cold glare. "I cannot imagine why you should think that any of your concern, Miss Ashley."

Annabelle, unused to the *ton*, stared at him in shock at the sharp set down before her temper flared. "My apologies, Your Grace, but my concern was for you, as it appeared you became unhappy at the mention of the lady's name. Thinking we were friends, I merely wished to help, but apparently offering friendship is a *faux pas* among the *ton*!" She spun her horse about. "I am sure your groom can escort me home."

The liveried young man accompanying them waited in confusion as the girl quickly rode off before the duke finally gestured him to follow.

Fortunately, the earl wasn't around when Annabelle strode back into the entry hall of Rothbury House, her eyes sparkling with unshed tears of frustration.

"Miss Annabelle, why are you back so early? Where is the duke?" Mrs. Gavin stared at her in surprise.

"Dukes! I wish I were back in Northumberland!"

"Oh, dear. Now whatever has happened? Come in here." She guided the distraught Annabelle to the small parlor and pulled on the cord for a servant. "Now, you sit here by the fire and compose yourself and tell me what has happened."

"Oh, Mrs. Gavin!" Annie gave in to the threatening tears as she poured out the morning's events. "Did I really do something so terribly wrong in worrying about him?" Annabelle sniffed.

"You did nothing wrong."

Both women started as the duke entered the room uninvited. "Will you excuse us, Mrs. Gavin?"

"Now, Your Grace, I don't think—" the housekeeper began huffily, but the duke interrupted.

"Please, madam. You may leave the door open for propriety's sake, but I wish to speak to Miss Ashley alone."

Annabelle stood, silently turning her back on the man as she dabbed in embarrassment at her eyes.

"Miss Ashley," the duke stiffly began when the housekeeper left, "I should explain I have had no experience with young women who—"

"Your Grace." Annabelle coolly turned to him. "I have already apologized. I fail to see why you should have found it necessary—"

"Oh, for heaven's sake, Annabelle. If you would but be quiet for a moment. I am trying to apologize to you!" the duke snapped impatiently.

As she stared at him he grinned wryly and added, "I fear I am not very adept at apologies."

"So it would appear," Annabelle replied, unable to restrain the answering grin.

"My dear girl." The duke laughingly pulled her against him for an impulsive hug. "Whyever aren't there more women like you?"

"May I inquire what is going on in here?"

The two guiltily sprang apart as the earl's icy voice interrupted the scene.

"I was merely apologizing to Annabelle, my friend. You need not worry," the duke hastened to explain.

"Annabelle, is it? Are you sure you are apologizing to the right person, my friend?" the earl angrily countered. "I would not have thought this of you, Heatherton."

"Richard, really. Charles was just—"

"Charles!" Richard roared as the duke rolled his eyes at Annabelle's unintentional slip.

"Oh, I'm sorry, Your Grace," she allowed with a quick smile at the duke before turning back to Richard. "I meant, the duke and I were only—"

"Miss Ashley, you shall go to your room immediately—and stay there until I send for you!" Richard demanded.

"Richard—"

"Now!"

"It's all right. Run along, my dear. I shall explain to your brother," the duke assured her, despite the earl's glare.

"Oh, men!" Annabelle sighed as she departed the room.

CHAPTER THIRTEEN

Annabelle, having not the least intention of allowing some autocratic male order her to her room, proceeded up to the nursery to check on the children.

"Annie! Annie!" She was greeted by a chorus of relieved young voices as she entered the room.

"Sit down, children," the new governess firmly ordered before turning to Annabelle. "We are in the middle of lessons, Miss Ashley. Was there something you needed?"

Annabelle drew her eyes from the pleading faces of the children with some effort. "Mrs. Thornton. I was not aware that you had arrived." She tried to keep her voice calm.

"I arrived over an hour ago. I believe you were out at the time," the governess advised, standing pointedly.

"Surely, you did not think we expected you to begin lessons today, Mrs. Thornton. You certainly must take some time to settle in and unpack."

"I had one of the serving girls unpack for me," the woman curtly declared. "I have always found it preferable with children to establish a firm routine as soon as possible. I am sure you will understand when I ask that it not be interrupted?"

"Of course." Annabelle struggled for control. "I merely came up to check on the children." She glanced about at the unhappy children Mrs. Thornton had seated separately about the room, forcibly reminding herself that she had promised Richard to give this woman a chance. "John David and Cecelia, where are they?"

"With the nanny, Miss Ashley. They are too young to be taught with this group. I will attend to them after lunch."

"Very well." Annabelle managed a comforting smile at the hopeful faces. "You children behave for Mrs. Thornton, and I will take you to the park this afternoon."

"Children should know to behave without being offered bribes," the woman haughtily declared. "I expect their lessons will take most of the afternoon to complete."

Annabelle's lips tightened. "I will be by for the children after lunch, Mrs. Thornton. They also need their exercise and fresh air."

The governess dared make no further comment as Annabelle angrily left in search of Sarah.

She found the nanny in her own room reading nursery tales to the two younger children. The woman started to stand as Annabelle lightly tapped on the open door. "Oh, Miss Annabelle, please come in."

"No, no, stay where you are." Annabelle waved her back to where she sat on the bed, a child cozily ensconced on either side.

"Hey, Annie," the two smaller children chimed in welcome, but unlike the other group, neither made a move toward her.

"Come listen." Cecelia invitingly patted the bed beside her. "Miss Sarah reads funny."

"Cecelia!" Annabelle began with a distressed glance at the older woman, but Sarah merely smiled.

"Cecelia is referring to my 'animal' voices, I believe," she explained.

"Miss Sarah can talk like a mouse, and like a cat, and even like a bird," John David declared in respectful tones.

"Oh, I see," Annabelle replied. "Well, I am glad to find at least some of the children enjoying themselves."

"You must have been by the nursery." Sarah gave her a cautious look.

"I'm afraid so. What do you think of Mrs. Thornton?"

"I don't like that mean teacher," Cecelia piped in. "She doesn't even smell nice like Miss Sarah." She buried her head against the woman's sleeve, sniffing appreciatively.

"I fear I am rather partial to making lilac sachets for clothes cupboards," Sarah explained, coloring slightly as Annabelle smiled. "And, on Mrs. Thornton, of course she hasn't spoken to me much, but she does seem—quite cultured."

"Oh, I am sure she was well-raised," Annabelle allowed, "but I meant, what do you think of her character?"

"Well, she must have had good references for His Lordship to have hired her?" Sarah carefully hedged.

Annabelle glanced at the children. "Why don't you two run down and see what kind of cookies that Cook is baking?"

"Cookies?" The two leapt up in unison.

"I like the new cook!" Cecelia declared over her shoulder as they raced out.

"Now, what do you really think of her?" Annabelle inquired casually, sitting down on the bedside. "Personally, I think she's liable to be much too hard on the children."

"Now, Miss Annabelle," Sarah declared fairly, "you know children do need a firm hand. Particularly those twins—Lord love them." She smiled. "I must admit she does seem a bit stern. I expect she just wants to establish authority with the children from the start so they will respect her."

"I hope you are right." Annabelle sighed. "I suppose I am just being overly protective."

Sarah smiled and nodded. "That possibility had also occurred to me, miss, but such feelings are quite normal when you love someone. You must quit your worrying and trust in the earl's judgement as to the children. I'm certain he isn't going to allow anyone to cause them harm."

"You are right, of course," Annabelle readily agreed before taking her leave.

As she returned to her own room, she considered Sarah's advice to trust that the earl wouldn't let anyone harm the children. The nanny had all but echoed Richard's own words. Annabelle smiled to herself on remembering how he had so comfortably held her in his arms when telling her that.

She had never even been close to an adult male before, and now in a matter of days had been held by two. But oddly, when the duke had hugged her it had seemed like being hugged by a brother. But when Richard, who was her brother—or at least step-brother—had held her it had felt altogether different. More than just comforting somehow.

"Miss Annabelle?"

Annabelle drew herself from her reverie and opened

the door to find Mrs. Cummings outside. "His Lordship asked if you would come take luncheon with him in the small dining room, miss. He wishes to speak with you."

"Oh, does he seem—angry about anything?" Annie questioned cautiously before committing herself.

"Angry?" The housekeeper looked at her curiously. "Why no. Rather, he seemed in a most pleasant mood."

"Really? Very well, I must change out of this riding habit, and then I will be right down."

Annabelle happily hummed to herself as she stripped off the blue habit and selected another of her new gowns, a simple yellow round gown, trimmed out in a soft cream Brussels lace. Her hair had become considerably windblown from the ride. She didn't wish to keep the earl waiting while she paged Brit to fix it back up for her. Rather, she just brushed it into glossy loose curls and tied it back with a yellow ribbon to match the dress.

Despite the housekeeper's assurances, Annabelle approached the small dining room with some trepidation.

The earl, however, turned from the window where he awaited her with a welcoming smile. "You need not look so hesitant. Come." He directed her to the seat where Barton stood solemnly holding her chair. "Charles managed to explain your, um, compromising position earlier—at least to a reasonable degree." He waited until the butler served them and left the room before continuing. "I really must caution you, however, that your attitude toward males is a bit—casual."

Annabelle avoided his eyes in sudden embarrassment. "I can understand that the situation looked rather suspect to you, my lord."

"Richard," the earl corrected. "Surely, if you can call the Duke of Heatherton 'Charles' on the second day of knowing him, you can call me Richard at home?"

Annabelle felt her cheeks flush. "I really did not intend to call the duke by his given name," she hastened to explain. "I just became flustered and it just rather—"

Richard chuckled. "You can cut line, my dear, I understand. However, I think you may do well to follow Lady Victoria's lead this evening in regard to decorum. If the two of you rub along well enough to become friends, I hope she can offer you guidance on the ways of the *ton*." He casually changed the subject. "Heatherton apologized for rounding on you for what he perceived an indiscretion, but he did not offer what the matter was about."

Annabelle didn't mind his oblique inquiry, as she hoped for some enlightenment on the matter herself. "Yes, I expect he told you we met the Countess Lieven in the park?"

At the earl's nod she continued.

"The duke had seemed to be in excellent humor. In fact, we were getting along rather well to that point, until the countess mentioned something about a Sophia Wellington having returned to town."

"Sophia Wellington?" the earl questioned. "Good heavens! That is Sophia Blairstone."

"Yes. The countess said this Sophia was residing at Blairstone Manor."

"Hmmm. And how did Charles greet the news that Sophia had returned to Blairstone?"

Richard listened in silence as Annabelle explained the duke's reaction to the countess's proposal. "But even after we finally continued our ride, the duke seemed quite distant. In fact, he scarcely noticed I was there."

"Surely you didn't ask him about Sophia?" The earl looked at her in disbelief.

"Well, yes," she reluctantly admitted. "He worried me. He seemed so—sad."

Richard considered her a moment in silence. "Annabelle, you are still quite young and have had little exposure to men. Although I can understand being sought out by a duke is a heady experience for a young woman, you must not allow your affections to become so readily involved."

"My affections? Oh, Richard, surely you don't imagine I'm developing a *tendre* for the man, or some such thing, merely because I worry about him? Actually, he seems even more like a brother than–" She stopped quickly and then moved on. "What was it about this Sophia that made him so angry?"

"It is old history. I had thought at the time it was more his pride injured than truly his heart," he mused almost to himself.

"So Sophia was someone he loved?" Annabelle had assumed as much.

"Apparently. She was quite beneath him, as Heatherton had recently come into the title when his father died, and Sophia was just a country baron's daughter, but that fact seemed to make little difference to Heatherton."

"So, what happened?" she insisted when he hesitated.

The earl raised a brow at her impatience but continued. "Sophia had arrived with her family to Blairstone that Season, apparently to buy wedding clothes to marry her childhood beau. That is when Heatherton met her and shocked the whole *ton* by offering for her scarcely two weeks later."

"And she turned him down?" Annabelle guessed.

"No. Apparently she was not too set on marrying Wellington at all. He was a neighboring baron's son and they had grown up together, so it was generally accepted they would marry. She told Heatherton she just needed time to gently break it off. But as it happened, the next thing we knew Wellington appeared and she was off to Gretna Green with him, leaving Heatherton with nothing but a brief note of apology.''

"The poor man!" Annabelle said. "But the countess said Sophia's husband was deceased so . . ."

"Annabelle, you are not to concern yourself further with this matter." Richard assumed he had put an end to the subject.

Annabelle went straight to the nursery on finishing her meal, knowing the children would have had luncheon earlier. As the governess had retired to her room for her own luncheon, Annabelle was met by none but a group of near militant siblings.

"Annabelle, I am not going to abide that horrid woman another day!" Elizabeth indignantly greeted her. "She treated me like I am some—some child in leading strings. And she doesn't know anything!"

"She wouldn't even let me and Thomas sit together!" Terry railed.

"She made me stand in the corner," a red-eyed Catherine sobbed, "just because I didn't do some stupid arithmetic the way she wanted."

"I don't want to 'tand in the corner and I don't know any 'withmetic!" Cecelia wailed in alarm, though she and John David hadn't even as yet had their lessons with the new governess.

Annabelle sighed. "Listen, why don't you all get your coats and we'll go into the park for a walk. That should make everyone feel better. Then we can talk about it."

Even the treat of the park, however, did little to raise the spirits of the group. It took Annabelle the full hour's walk to even convince the children to agree to give the woman another chance. "We must trust Richard's decision on Mrs. Thornton. We all know he is trying to do his best for us," Annabelle argued, though she herself was becoming more and more unhappy about his choice of governess.

On returning, Annabelle decided she would just insist on sitting in on lessons that afternoon to see how this woman was going about teaching. Unfortunately her plans were thwarted, as they no sooner returned to the town house than a rather pretentious carriage pulled up.

"Lady St. Claire and the Misses Barbara and Lucille await you in the parlor, Miss Annabelle." Barton caught her just as she was heading up the stairs.

Annabelle looked askance at the butler on hearing gay giggles erupt from the room. "Who are they?" she whispered, but the butler merely offered an elegant shrug in reply.

"Shall I have Mrs. Cummings send a tea tray, my lady?"

"Good heavens, must we?" Annabelle sighed.

The merest hint of a sympathetic smile broke the staid Barton's impeccable composure. "I expect so, Miss Annabelle. I shall see to it right away."

"Oh, my dear Miss Ashley, I could not wait another day to welcome you and your dear brother, the earl, to town." A rather alarming-sized, lavender-gowned matron descended upon Annabelle the moment she entered the room. "And these are my dear, dear daughters, Barbara and Lucille. They have been so excited about meeting you. Haven't you, dears?"

The two young girls agreed with delighted giggles,

though oddly both seemed more interested in watching the door.

Annabelle found herself glancing back at the door in curiosity. "I am quite pleased to meet you, Lady—" She managed to stumble through the names. When she finished the greetings and had invited the ladies to be seated, an awkward silence fell with everyone foolishly smiling at one another.

"Well," Annabelle said, trying to evince polite interest, "I expect this is the first Season for you?" She smiled at the girls.

"Oh, yes." They delightedly giggled before sinking back into smiling silence, carefully watching the door.

Annabelle glanced somewhat worriedly at the door. Perhaps they were thirsty and hoping for tea? Surely, that was it.

"I expect you have been on morning calls all day?"

"Oh, yes," They giggled and again sank back into watchful smiles.

"I shall ring for a tea tray." Annabelle decided to try for temporary escape from the strain, though Barton had already ordered it. She had barely reached the cord before a knock sounded at the door.

"Oh! Perhaps that's the earl joining us!" Lady St. Claire excitedly clapped her hands, her daughters giggling, directing their smiles at the doorway.

The parlor maid looked in concern at the vanishing smiles on the guests' faces as she entered with the tea tray.

"Well. Now that was quick!" Annabelle brightly declared, releasing the bellpull, to the young maid's further confusion.

"Shall I stay and pour, miss?"

"No—no, you may go on," Annabelle dismissed her, needing something to do to fill the bizarre visit. She made much ceremony of pouring into the fine porcelain cups. "And are you in London just for the Season, Lady St. Claire?" She tried frantically to begin a conversation.

"Yes, for the Season," the lady agreed with a smile and reached for a scone.

"That's nice." Annabelle smiled and again sipped her tea. "And Barbara, you and Lucille, you are enjoying London?"

"Oh yes," they agreed amidst giggles, with eyes still firmly set on the door.

Everyone smiled as silence fell. "Here, you girls have not had any scones." Annabelle reached for the plate to offer them each one.

"Oh no!" their mama decreed. "We must watch our figures, now mustn't we, dears?"

The girls agreed with proper giggles, though their eyes had moved briefly from the door to the platter where their mother, notwithstanding the "we," delicately gathered up yet another of the scones.

"It is quite lovely weather today, isn't it?" Annabelle asked, smiling more urgently.

"Oh, much too sunny!" Lady St. Claire declared in horror through a mouthful of pastry. "I almost feared to bring the dear girls out in it. We must be so careful of our complexions, mustn't we, girls?"

The giggles gaily agreed, and Annabelle distractedly reached for a scone herself, wondering how long it would be before these strange creatures left.

"Oh, my heavens!" To her amazement Lady St. Claire moved the plate from Annabelle's reach. "Why, we have almost finished off all of these wonderful pastries! Whatever shall His Lordship think of us, if we don't save him one?"

"I doubt the earl will even know," Annabelle smiled tightly, "as he is out at the moment."

"Out? Did you say out?" The lady stared in dismay. "The earl is not at home?"

"Not at home?" the girls echoed, their eyes uncomprehendingly darting from the door to their mother.

"Well. Come along, dears." The lavender lady briskly stood. "We must not take up all of dear Miss Ashley's day now, must we?"

The girls agreed, and their giggles echoed down the hallway as Barton staidly opened the door for them.

Annabelle sighed in relief as she heard the front door close and wearily headed once again toward the stairs. It was really time to begin preparing for the theater that evening, as she needed to bathe and shampoo her hair.

"Barton?"

"Yes, Miss Annabelle?"

"Could you have someone bring my bath up?"

"Yes, miss," the butler answered, but at that moment the knocker loudly rattled again at the door.

Barton turned glancing out the door's side windows. "Miss, I do fear it is more callers."

"Oh, no!" Annabelle froze in horror.

The butler helpfully offered, "Are you at home?"

She looked at him in confusion, and he elucidated, "I mean, Miss Annabelle, are you at home to the callers?"

"Barton, are you saying I don't have to be at home?" she asked in delighted amazement.

Barton restrained a smile. "Yes, miss. It is quite acceptable to be not at home to callers when one is otherwise occupied."

"You are simply beyond wonderful! Yes, I am not at

home—or, no, I am not at home—whichever. Just send them away, please!"

"Yes, miss." The butler turned away to hide his chuckles, discreetly waiting until Annabelle had fled up the stairs before he opened the door.

CHAPTER FOURTEEN

Annabelle leaned back in the ornately curved tub in pleasure. She had thought her days were busy at the castle, but it seemed here she'd scarcely had a moment to herself.

"Are you ready for me to shampoo your hair, miss?" Brit came over to her.

"Oh, thank you, yes." She sat up allowing the maid to carefully pour a pitcher of warm water over her hair.

"It is such a pleasure to have someone to help me with this awful mass," Annabelle commented as the girl massaged the soap in. "I have so often been tempted to just cut it off rather than trying to handle it alone."

"Oh, miss, you must never!" Brit declared aghast. "You have such lovely thick hair. I have some delightful little shell pins I'm going to pin it up with tonight that shall go wonderful with that sea green gown you are wearing."

Annabelle listened in relaxed contentment to Brit's happy chatter as she finished her hair and wrapped her warmly in a robe to sit before the fire.

Brit busily toweled most of the water from her hair before positioning her on the settee. "Now you can lay back there, and I can bring you a magazine or book if you like."

"Actually, I think I would rather just rest for a minute

or two," Annabelle said as the maid carefully arrayed her hair over the side of the settee toward the cheery flames.

"This will speed the drying. Now, miss, you just lay there. I need to carry out these pitchers and fetch someone to pick up the bath. I'll be back shortly."

As Brit left, Annabelle stretched her legs out on the settee and closed her eyes. She was just drifting off to sleep when a light knock sounded at the door.

"You may come in," she called sleepily, not even opening her eyes, assuming it to be the maid returning or servants coming for the bath.

The earl stood for long moments, unable to bring himself to disturb the tranquil scene before him. Annabelle's wealth of raven locks were touched with dancing reds and blues from the firelight where they cascaded over the sofa's arm. Though the softness of her body was concealed beneath the robe, the garment ended some inches above the very pleasingly curved ankles and delightfully small, narrow feet.

Richard smiled as her toes flexed sensually. "Are you awake?"

Annabelle's eyes flew open in surprise at the male voice. "Richard! What are you doing here?"

"You did say come in?"

"Oh, good heavens." Annabelle quickly sat up, carefully holding the robe's edges together as she sought to tie it shut. "I had thought you to be Brit or one of the other maids."

The earl sat down in the fireside chair, and casually crossed his legs as he watched her fuss.

Annabelle finally got the robe tied to her satisfaction and glanced up. "You could at least have turned your back!" she quarrelsomely declared. Then following his gaze down to her still-exposed ankles, she tucked them under the settee's edge. "Richard, you're my brother." She glared in indignation.

"Step-brother," he modified with a slow grin.

At her startled glance, Richard could not restrain a chuckle as he wryly advised, "I owe you a few uncomfortable moments at least."

"What do you mean?" Annie cautiously asked.

The earl brought out the thick stack of sheets covered in her neat handwriting.

"Oh, that's the—list of repairs?"

"Yes. The list of repairs—where you were writing down *my* instructions. Though oddly now that Smythe brings me the costs broken down item by item, there are quite a number of things I cannot seem to recall ordering."

"You can't recall?"

"No, I can't."

"Oh. Well, it was some time ago. It is perfectly natural that you wouldn't remember everything," Annabelle said, busying herself with an errant thread on the robe's sash.

"Annabelle."

"Yes?"

She managed to meet his steady gaze for but a moment before rushing into explanations. "Well, it was just that you couldn't—I mean you shouldn't—be expected to totally detail the renovations, so I just, well, added what I expected you might have overlooked." Her hopeful smile wavered under the earl's steady gaze.

"Hmm, let's see." Richard glanced at the sheets. "Ah, yes, of course. It seems I definitely forgot 'peacock blue Etruscan tiles for the ante-chamber into the north wing.'"

"They shall look quite elegant," Annabelle assured him.

"I should hope so, considering the cost," he dryly replied, naming the figure off the order sheets.

"My heavens! I had no idea. I saw some like that at the Prince's pavilion in Brighton and—"

"Good God. Prinny's pavilion!"

Annabelle jumped at his roar. "Well, yes. I—"

"Annabelle, the Prince Regent is about to bankrupt all of England with his extravagances of decor, and you expect I can match him?"

"It was but a few tiles!"

The earl glared at her. "I hope you did not use the Prince as your standard in any further selections." At her silence he looked up sharply.

"Well—" She hesitated.

"What?"

"Merely, some wallpaper that was particularly lovely—"

"Ah, doubtless the twelve bolts of oriental embossed silk paper 'Birds of the World'?"

"It took all of twelve bolts?" she asked weakly.

"For a room nine by seven meters? Where in the name of heaven were you putting it?" He glanced at the sheets. "The nursery? Good God, woman!"

"It is bright and pretty. Children need bright and pretty things about them to—to develop cheerful natures. And with all the birds it will be very—educational."

The earl shook his head in disbelief.

"Well, if you don't like my additions, you can always just scratch them off!" Annabelle impatiently sighed.

"Smythe had already sent the order in."

"Whyever did you let him order these items if you didn't wish them?"

The earl hesitated. "Actually, I never managed to find time to read over the sheets," he reluctantly admitted. "I just gave them to him." At her raised brows, he snapped, "I assumed I could trust you to have put down what I said!"

"Oh dear!" Annabelle gave him a guilty look.

"Oh dear, indeed!" The earl glared. "You have added a small fortune to my intended costs!"

"Now that is simply not true!" Annabelle indignantly defended herself. "As a matter of fact, I am quite sure it will balance out in your favor considering the things I took off that you wanted to do."

"What?" the earl roared.

"Oh, for heaven's sake. Would you quit yelling so? Here, I'll show you." Annabelle, forgetting about her precarious state of dress, moved over to kneel beside his chair and began flipping peremptorily through the sheets in his lap. "See. Right here for instance"—she pointed—"you would have had me list that this entire fireplace be demolished and newly rebuilt. But it is completely faced with hand-painted Italian tiles. You can't even buy those anymore at any price—not to mention that you would have had to purchase something else to face it with. I believe you had told me to list marble. So on that alone I probably saved the cost of the wallpaper—not to mention preserving a priceless heirloom! And on this page—remember that carved oak paneling in the colonnade?"

Richard felt the warmth of her body through the robe like a fire on his thigh where she leaned against him. Her hair had fanned out over his hand on the armrest as she bent over. He turned his hand and wonderingly closed it over a still-damp cluster of thick, silken curls, barely stopping himself from raising the mass to more closely appreciate the sweet scent that had enveloped him when she knelt.

"And on this solid oak flooring, why there was no good reason in the world to—"

One of the sheets slipped loose, and Annabelle reached across him to grab it.

The earl stifled a groan as he momentarily felt the soft pressure of her breast against his thigh. "Annabelle—" He desperately tried to keep his voice level.

"Now, on courtyard's paving stones—you are probably right that they couldn't be matched. Then again, you can still use these and just make a pattern of contrasting ones, rather than buy all new."

As her fingers flipping through the bottom sheets brushed over his leg, Richard sharply drew his breath in. "Annabelle," he tried again evenly, "if you don't mind, would you—"

"So," she finished, triumphantly smiling up at him. "Now even you must admit that, weighing it all out, I have probably even saved you money."

The earl, who couldn't have repeated a word she'd said had his very life depended on it, found himself admitting agreement in a surprisingly calm voice.

"Thank you, Richard. I just knew you would understand when I explained." Annabelle laughed in relief.

The earl sighed when her slim fingers closed warmly over his knee as she pushed herself up to stand.

"Oh, dear." Annabelle stopped halfway. "I do believe my hair has somehow become entangled in your signet ring!"

Richard forced his fingers to release the cluster of curls and found that indeed several locks had managed to twine themselves about his heavy ring. "Here, let me help." He stood with momentary relief, only to find himself still much too close to her.

"Ouch, wait! Be still," Annabelle complained as he tried to move away. "You're pulling my hair. Let me." She caught his right hand and began carefully unwinding the long strands, oblivious to the fact that her stance allowed the robe to gape open in a very improper area.

The earl felt his temples pounding as his gaze revealed a glimpse of soft ivory breast barely concealed behind a cascade of raven locks.

Instinctively, his left hand had just begun to move up to brush aside the annoying curls, when Brit reentered the room.

"Miss Annabelle, I have brought some— Your Lordship?" She stopped in surprise.

Annabelle glanced around. "Brit? It's all right. Do come on in." She laughed at the girl's expression. "We were just going over these sheets of repairs, and this ridiculous mop of hair of mine somehow managed to get tangled about Richard's ring— Ah, there. Now it's loose." She moved back in satisfaction. Happily, her movement closed the gaping robe.

"Good heavens! Just look at the time, and my hair isn't even completely dry. Did you want anything else, Richard?"

The earl blinked. "Oh, no. I will—leave you to your dressing."

CHAPTER
FIFTEEN

It was Victoria's first time at the theater, as well as Annabelle's, since Victoria had only recently emerged from the school room. She and Annabelle were both enthralled with the pageantry as they entered the packed ante-chamber.

"Look, the Prince himself is here tonight!" Vicky excitedly whispered, as she pointed out an ornately arrayed gentleman of rather large proportions in the center of a exclusive group. "And he has Mrs. Fitzherbert even! Isn't this exciting?"

"Who is Mrs. Fitzherbert?"

"You goose!" Vicky giggled. "She is the Prince's light o' love! Everyone knows that! Oh look, it's Beau Brummel with the Prince."

"Who is the tall man and the lovely woman with the red hair?" asked Annabelle.

Richard replied, "That's Gareth St. John, Earl of Cantonly, and his new countess, Lady Jessica. It is said that they have just returned from their wedding trip on the Continent."

Annabelle wistfully watched the couple join a small group of well-wishers.

"Oh, isn't it magnificent," Victoria continued. "Why, everyone is here tonight."

"Heatherton! Haven't seen you here before, old man,"

remarked an "exquisite" of the Corinthian set as he approached the duke. To the girls' amazement, he raised a jeweled quizzing glass to one eye and peered at them. "And what delightful young ladies!"

The duke obliged him, performing the necessary introductions. "Viscount Mancell, my sister Lady Victoria and Miss Annabelle Ashley, the sister of the Earl of Rothbury."

Victoria and Annabelle exchanged covert grins as the puce-clad young gentleman gracefully bent over their hands before turning his attention to Richard. "Ah, Dunne. Welcome back. Haven't seen you since we were at Eton together. Why, my good fellow," he jovially continued, turning his quizzing glass on Richard's formal black cutaway, "you must allow me to introduce you to my tailor."

Richard barely had time to counter the two girls' gleeful looks with a baleful glare before their group was converged upon by a wave of the curious *ton* seeking introductions.

Annabelle's head seemed to be swimming, so asea was it with the names of Lord this and Lady that. She hadn't the least possibility of keeping them all separate.

"We really must be departing to our box," the duchess finally announced, and began to move off. Most of the group about them took the hint and turned to head to their own seats, but one woman still pushed forward. "Your Grace, excuse me but I simply must speak a moment to the earl."

The duchess impatiently stopped. "Mrs. Rothschild," she acknowledged with a nod. "Lord Dunne, the Earl of Rothbury," she said, and as Annabelle was currently holding his arm she continued. "And Miss Annabelle Ashley, the earl's sister."

The woman looked sharply at Annabelle. "Miss Ashley," she acknowledged before continuing. "We have not before met, my lord, but I know your family. In fact, my older sister, Matilda, was your late father's wife."

"My condolences on your sister's demise, madam," the earl politely offered.

"And likewise on your father's, my lord. I could not resist the chance to inquire on how Matilda's dear children are faring. Did I not hear that they are residing in London with you?"

The earl's eyes narrowed at some indefinable false note in her statement. "We are all residing in London at the moment while Dunne Castle is under renovation," he curtly explained. "As for the children, they are both quite well, thank you." He nodded in dismissal, but the woman continued.

"And Miss Ashley is your sister? Why, I was certain Matilda told me the late earl had only older sons?"

Richard impatiently sighed. "My step-sister, Mrs. Rothschild. Now you must excuse us, I fear the curtain is just now rising."

None of them thought anymore of Mrs. Rothschild and her questions as they enjoyed the play. It was only the next day that the dowager duchess began to worry on hearing that Mrs. Rothschild had been asking quite a few questions of whomever she could corner about the earl and his family. As Charles had ridden out early to check on one of the family estates, the duchess decided to pay a morning call on Annabelle and the earl.

Annabelle quickly came down to the parlor on hearing who was calling. "Your Grace." She curtsied prettily to the older woman. "Vicky! What a lovely surprise that you have dropped by."

"Thank you my dear." The duchess smiled. "Actually, Victoria has pestered me to death to bring her to see the dress you shall be wearing to Almack's tonight, but I also wished to speak to Lord Dunne."

"Your Grace, Lady Victoria," the earl greeted the ladies as he entered the parlor a few moments later. "Barton said you wished to speak with me, Your Grace?"

"If you don't mind. Annabelle, dear, why don't you take Victoria up to see your gown?"

Richard politely stood waiting until the girls left the room.

"Do sit down, Richard." The duchess smiled up at him. "It is difficult to believe you have grown so tall. And an earl, yet! It seems only the other day that you and Charles were running about in nappies!"

Richard chuckled as he seated himself. "Did Annabelle ring for tea?"

The duchess dismissively waved a hand. "No, thank you, we really cannot remain long. There was just a matter that concerned me about last night."

"At the theater?"

"Yes. You recall that woman, Mrs. Rothschild?"

"Quite a determined lady, I must say," the earl wryly noted.

"A meddling marplot is what she is!" The duchess sniffed. "And you are quite right about her determination. I have heard from various of my friends that she was making all manner of inquiries about you and Annabelle at the theater last night."

Richard raised his brows. "That is interesting. She said she was the sister of my father's late wife. I fear I never met Lady Matilda. Do you know much of the family?"

"Oh, yes indeed. The Rothschilds hold a baronetcy. At one time quite a respected title, but apparently the last heirs were addicted to gambling. Now from what I hear, they haven't a feather to fly with."

"Hmm," the earl considered. "Well, I cannot think what mischief she could make. I shouldn't expect she has any particular influence to carry it out even if she planned something?"

"That is not entirely true. Though they are of no fortune, she does have some rather strong influences. As it happens, she is hand and glove with Mrs. Fitzherbert, and you know how the Prince caters to her!"

"Yes, now that could be a problem. But what would you think she may be about?"

"The two younger children, perhaps, as they are of her family?"

The earl shook his head. "I shouldn't think it. The family didn't seem at all interested in John David and Cecelia when Father died. In fact, according to the solicitor, they made it quite plain that they would assume no responsibility."

The duchess raised her brows, considering. "I do recall some talk of that. I wonder. You do realize that your father became—well, rather eccentric with age?" she gently questioned.

"You need not dissemble, Your Grace. From the state of affairs I have discovered, I expect Father was a total Bedlamite in his latter years," Richard dryly allowed.

"Hmm. Well, it was rumored in the *ton* that he had quite impoverished the earldom. Personally, knowing a bit more than most would of the estate entailments of Rothbury, I could not fathom that such was even possible."

"Fortunately not. Though had it been, Father probably

would have lost the lot of it. His last man of business alone managed to make off with a small fortune!"

"Such a pity!" The duchess shook her head. "But I was thinking, as pinch-pursed as this Rothschild family is, had they thought the earldom of any worth, they would have likely sought guardianship of the children simply for the use of their inheritance."

"I believe I see your direction," Richard acknowledged in a most serious tone. "Now word has doubtless gotten about that there is blunt to be had, so you are thinking they might be trying to find some way into the earldom's coffers?"

"Precisely. And knowing that Rothschild woman, she would sink to any level to achieve her gains."

"I hope this Mrs. Rothschild is aware that there is no possibility of her taking the children from my keeping!"

The duchess suppressed a smile at the lord's vehemence. "Why, Richard, I seem to recall rumor was that you were none too pleased at having to return from the Indies to take over this duty."

The earl had the grace to color under the lady's penetrating gaze. "I must confess to such feelings initially, but I assure you it was only from never having known the children. They are now my family and, as such, under my protection. I will not allow anyone to cause them upset."

"But what shall become of them when you return to captain your ship?"

"I can see Heatherton has been discussing my plans," the earl remarked rather testily.

"He is my son." The duchess shrugged. "Mothers can always manage to find out what they wish, but I don't think you answered the question."

The earl sighed, feeling much the young lad taken to

task. "I will not return to the sea until I have all of Rothbury's affairs in order, including the children under proper care and estate matters resolved with my steward and solicitors."

"Leave?" Terry looked in horror at his twin where the two crouched against the doorway listening. As soon as they had seen Annabelle and Victoria upstairs, they had determined it would be much jollier to go down and see if the duke might have come along. "Richard is going to leave us?"

"I can't believe it!" Thomas cried in shock.

"Shhh." Terry pressed his ear back to the crack as the conversation continued.

"The children under proper care, Richard? Like a governess and nannies?"

"Your Grace," the earl gently reminded, "I am no longer the lad running about in nappies, you recall. I am quite capable of handling my own affairs. But as you seem concerned, I will allow that I have determined to place the *Southwind* on a new trade route to France and Belgium so that I will be home more often. And Annabelle will, of course, be with the children."

The duchess raised a brow. "My apologies, my lord. As Charles must often remind me, I fear I tend to fall back into the mother role. I would be first to admit you have done an admirable job, particularly under the circumstance of your surprise family. It does please me that you have determined to remain closer to home, though I must still question the advisability of any extended absence of the only adult family member."

Richard gave an impatient sigh. "As I mentioned, Annabelle—"

"My dear Richard," the duchess interrupted, "have you paid no attention to your sister? She is a beautiful, as well as delightful, young woman, a fact which your peers have not missed—including my own son, I might add. You can scarcely expect it will be long before she is wed and setting up her own nursery."

The earl became very still for a moment. "You are, I expect, correct. This is not a matter I have put to any serious thought."

"Whatever are you boys doing down here?" At that moment they heard Annabelle's lightly chastising voice outside the parlor door. "Aren't you supposed to be in the classroom?"

"They certainly are!" advised another much more stern voice, and the protesting youngsters were taken away.

Annabelle and Victoria entered the parlor after lightly rapping. "I fear we have thoroughly discussed all of both Annabelle's and my own gowns, Mother," Victoria archly declared. "So if you are not yet finished with your private discussion, there is nothing for it but that the two of us must be off to Bond Street for some new items of conversation."

"Heaven forbid!" The duchess rose in mock horror. "Bond Street already knows you all too well. 'Tis a wonder the modistes don't drop by for tea as it is. Come along, dear, we do have other calls."

After they left, Annabelle turned to Richard, smiling. "That whole family is so absolutely delightful—" She noted his look and stopped. "Richard, is something wrong?"

The earl drew his thoughts away from the surprisingly painful vision of Annabelle as his friend's new duchess.

"Oh, it is nothing with which you need concern yourself. I have checked with the stable," he continued, changing the subject, "and the cattle I purchased have been delivered. I had thought perhaps you and the children might enjoy riding over with me to see them this afternoon."

"Oh, Richard, we would love to." She ran over and impulsively hugged him. "You are absolutely the most wonderful brother."

Oddly, the compliment gave the earl little pleasure.

CHAPTER SIXTEEN

The children seemed unnaturally subdued as they filed out to the earl's coach after luncheon. The earl raised an inquiring brow to Annabelle, but she merely shrugged, as mystified as he.

"Do you really think we can all manage in just one coach, Richard?" Annabelle doubtfully glanced into the interior, as he helped Cathy up to the step.

"It isn't far," replied the earl. "See, if Ceci shares a spot with me we shall all fit quite nicely." He demonstrated by placing the delighted youngest child in his lap.

Annabelle squeezed in beside him and the earl tapped on the roof for the coachmen to be off.

Once the coach lurched into action, the children seemed to forget whatever had been dampening their mood and began plying the earl with eager questions on their mounts.

As the relentless children elicited pony sizes and colors, Annabelle found herself distracted by the warmth of the earl's body pressed shoulder to thigh against her in the cramped confines. He had placed his arm on the seat behind her to provide a bit more room, and she determined it to be very pleasant to allow her head to rest ever so accidentally against the hard muscle of his shoulder.

"Now dear, you will muss Richard's neckcloth."

Annabelle caught Cecelia's small hand as she buried it exploringly into the elaborate folds his valet had labored over.

"I'm sorry–" the child began, but Richard stopped her.

"Don't worry, my sweet." The earl playfully tousled the child's curls. "Monfort has despaired of my ever returning with one of the blamed things intact."

As the earl turned his attention back to a question John David asked, the child lay her head contentedly against his chest.

Annabelle found herself assailed by something strongly akin to jealousy as she watched the lord's long fingers unconsciously stroking Cecelia's hair.

"You haven't told us what color Annie's horse is," Elizabeth reminded the earl as for the third time he listed the purchases.

"Hmmm. Haven't I?"

Annabelle blushed as the earl smiled down at her.

"Now what color horse do you think Annie should have?" he teasingly questioned the children.

"Blue is her favorite color!" Cecelia declared. "Isn't it, Annie?"

"You gudgeon!" Thomas laughed. "Horses don't come in blue."

"Well, now—you mustn't be so sure." Richard chuckled, thinking Annabelle's locks were of such dark blackness as to have almost bluish tints.

The conversation was brought to a halt as the carriage pulled into the stable yard and the children excitedly piled out.

The stable ostlers, previously alerted, had a row of beribboned ponies saddled and awaiting the awestruck children.

Happy pandemonium reigned as Richard and Annabelle helped John David and Cecelia onto shaggy, plump Shetlands, to be carefully led about by the stable hands. Annabelle couldn't restrain a teasing grin at the earl as Cathy was indeed led to a silky brown-spotted pony. "That one was a bit of a problem," Richard quipped. "I feared for a while there I might have to resort to a paint brush."

"We are not babies!" Their attention was demanded by the twins, who were indignantly refusing assistance in mounting their ponies, and Richard and Annabelle walked over.

"We wish to ride the ponies alone!" Terry grandly demanded.

"They have ridden?" the earl questioned Annabelle quietly before nodding permission for the concerned grooms to allow the boys to excitedly clamber onto a pair of perfectly matched black Shetlands.

"Oh, Richard! She's so very lovely." Elizabeth breathed as a delicately dappled, small mare was led over to her. "Oh, young man—" Annabelle and Richard exchanged an amused look as the girl haughtily gestured to an admiring young groom to help her into the sidesaddle.

Annabelle slipped her hand into the earl's almost unconsciously as they stood for a moment watching the children. "This day you have truly made six children ecstatic, my lord!" She laughed up at him.

Richard teasingly raised her hand to his lips as he bowed. "My pleasure. But come, and let me see how I have done with the seventh—child."

Annabelle wrinkled her nose at his designation, but eagerly allowed him to lead her into the roomy, cobbled barn.

A soft whicker greeted them as Richard led her over to a box stall. "Her name is Arabesque."

Annabelle drew her breath in as the horse's delicately shaped head of ebony silk pushed through the stall door to sniff at her hand. "Arabesque," she softly repeated the name. "Richard, she's beautiful!" She gently touched the mare's satin nose. "Oh please, can we bring her out so I can see her?"

Annabelle stared speechless as the mare gracefully pranced from the stall. "I have never seen any animal so wonderful! What is her breed?"

"She's an Arabian. There are not too many of them in England." Richard smiled as Annabelle moved over to stroke the mare's silken coat in awe.

"Richard—I—"

His smile vanished in alarm as he saw her eyes fill with tears. "Annie, what is wrong?" He tossed the mare's lead to the nearby groom and moved quickly toward her.

"Oh, Richard—"

The earl stopped in amazement as she flung herself laughing and crying at the same time into his arms.

"Nothing's wrong! I just can't believe—she's so—I can't believe you bought me something so absolutely magnificent!"

Richard laughed in relief as he enfolded her in his arms. "You silly puss! Does this mean then that you like the beast?" He raised her face, wiping the tears tenderly from her cheeks.

Annabelle slipped her arms around his neck and raising up on tiptoes kissed his cheek. "I love her."

The earl's arms momentarily tightened about her before he recalled himself, and forcing a smile, set her away from him. "I have arranged for the stable to bring her by in the morning along with Saxon. I'll ride with you out in the country so you can become accustomed to her.'' He carefully turned away. ''I'm afraid we should probably be returning now, if you're to have time to get dressed for Almack's tonight.''

Annabelle happily laughed as she went over to hug the mare's delicate arched neck. ''I was so excited about the ball at Almack's before, but now I can't wait until tomorrow.''

Later in his library, the earl stared unseeing at the sheaves of accounts he had intended going over. For days he had fought with growing alarm the feelings Annabelle had innocently aroused. ''The child is your sister!'' he growled to an uncaring ink pot. That is, of course, not true, his wayward thoughts curtly corrected. She is no kin at all and certainly not a child! It is just the proximity, he finally convinced himself. After the ball tonight, she would doubtless have all manner of suitors to occupy her time, and seeing less of her was all he needed. He vaguely considered the courting of some other woman to dispel his thoughts. The idea, however, was displeasing. He insisted to himself that he had no desire to marry and of course could not trifle with some young lady's feeling without serious intent.

Heatherton had suggested introducing him to several new and delightful members of the *demi-monde*, but that had even less appeal.

What he needed was to turn his mind to settling the estate as quickly as was feasible and taking his proper place at the helm of the *Southwind*. The earl decisively reached for a quill. He would immediately post a letter to be put on a packet to Jamaica summoning his flagship home.

"My lord, Mr. Smythe has returned," Barton advised him.

"Good. Send him in." The earl considered the letter to his captain a moment and then added a paragraph. Marissa and her family would have good use of the large home he had resided in when in Jamaica. He allowed himself a minute's reflection on the dusky beauty before decisively sealing the letter. The property, plus the sum of money he'd directed the captain to pay her, would make her quite wealthy. He smiled—knowing his resourceful mistress, she would doubtless manage quite well.

"Robert"—he handed the missive to his steward—"have this sent to Southampton to be put on the *Monarch*," he named another of his packets, "when she docks next week."

"Of course, my lord." The steward carefully put the letter with his other papers. "I have dispatched the first wagons to Northumberland, as you directed, and believe everything is in order so that I may depart with the ones leaving today, if you have no other wish."

"That is excellent. You have found enough workers?"

"Oh yes, my lord," he assured him. "There are more than enough men about London eager for work. Especially when it includes lodging and food."

"Very good. I have had a good portion of beef, fowl, and grains redirected from the home farms to the castle, so you should not have a problem with feeding the workers. Have you a schedule as yet for the repairs?"

"Based on your assessments, my lord, I expect there shall be no problem in having the main halls in order within the three months you have allowed. Of course, rebuilding the older wing will take longer. Nonetheless, with the number of workers you've allotted, I believe we can have the outer structure finished before winter calls a halt to the exterior building."

Richard nodded in satisfaction. "I shall probably be up toward the end of the month to see your progress."

After his steward's departure, he found he was quite looking forward to returning to Northumberland. The *Southwind* should be back in port by then and he could sail her up the coast. He needed to survey the small harbor outside the old wing.

A short while later, Richard watched Annabelle descend the stairway in an odd silence. "Do I look sufficient for Almack's?" she worriedly asked.

"Sufficient? My dear, you are absolutely beautiful!"

Annabelle felt a startling warmth rush through her as Richard took her hand and raised it to his lips.

"I am not certain I should allow you to go," the earl lightly remarked, marshaling his thoughts. "I shall doubtless be besieged by young gallants pounding at my door by dawn."

Annabelle covered her discomposure with a light laugh. "You will probably encourage them to take me off your hands when you get the modiste's bill for this gown." She twirled before him.

The earl's eyes darkened as the silver threads of the white gauze shimmered like stars beneath the candelabra. "I have already received the bill for that gown, brat!" he advised her. "But had determined to restrain comment until the viewing."

"Oh." She cautiously looked at him. "You have?"

"In this case, I cannot but consider it money well spent." He smiled, offering his arm as he forcefully kept his gaze from the smooth, pearly skin exposed at the gown's decolletage. "Come, the carriage is waiting."

Annabelle could not help but be aware of the stir they

caused on entering the famed halls of Almack's. It seemed everyone near became suddenly hushed.

Feeling Annabelle's tension, Richard smiled down at her, patting her hand. "The *ton* is always curious of newcomers," he softly advised. "Ah, here come Heatherton and Lady Victoria."

Richard had a difficult time concealing the irrational surge of jealousy at the warmth with which the duke greeted Annabelle. "Miss Ashley"—he lingeringly raised her hand to his lips—"your beauty puts every other woman here in the pale!"

"Charles!" Victoria teasingly protested.

"Except my lovely sister, of course," he quickly added.

"Vicky, you do look lovely," Annabelle assured her. "Doesn't she, Richard?" She found herself, however, oddly disconcerted at the look of complete agreement she caught in Richard's eyes as he bent over the younger girl's hand.

They scarcely had time to exchange further pleasantries before they were surrounded. Eager mamas rushed blushing young debutantes over for the rare chance of presenting them to both the duke and this new impressive young earl. Only slightly less obvious were Richard's and Charles's peers, sauntering over to sign the dance cards of these two stunning, not to mention wealthy, additions to the *ton*.

Annabelle's head was soon aching from the countless inanities of trivial talk and felt as though her face must be frozen in a perpetual smile, when with relief she saw the duke approaching her for the dinner dance he had marked on her card.

"My dear, should I be flattered by such a look of

welcome?" he teasingly said, taking her arm to lead her to where the quadrille was forming.

"Only, Your Grace, if I may count on your not offering to write odes to my eyebrows or trying to discover by oblique means how much of a dowry Richard intends settling on me!"

The duke pretentiously raised his quizzing glass. "Hmmm, delightful eyebrows indeed." He tucked away the glass with a sigh. "But sadly, I have no talent with odes. However, on this other matter, exactly how much did you say the earl was—?"

Richard at that moment happened to notice the pair and felt a sharp pang at the teasing interchange he witnessed.

"Ah, your friend the duke seems quite taken with your sister," Lord Braston innocently remarked, and was amazed when Richard gave him a very cold look and curtly turned away.

After the dance, as Annabelle departed to the dining hall on the duke's arm, she smiled up at him. "It shall feel so good to be able to sit down for a few moments."

He archly raised a brow. "Am I to conclude that to be a comment on my dancing?"

Annabelle laughed. "I seem to recall, sir, that it was I who stepped upon your foot in that last exchange, for which I must offer my apology."

"Ah." The duke chuckled. "Not at all. I shall forever treasure the memories of that featherlike touch with your silver slipper even unto—"

Annabelle, giggling at his fanciful soliloquy as they walked, was surprised to sense the duke suddenly stiffen. She followed his gaze across the room, where it appeared frozen on that of a graceful young matron.

The duke noted Annabelle following his look and

abruptly turned away. "Here, why don't you sit over here, and I will bring our plates?" He gave her no time to comment as he departed.

Annabelle watched the duke in concern as he prepared the plates, very carefully keeping his back to the other woman. The woman also seemed to be making a concerted effort to keep her eyes on her companions, but Annabelle cold not miss the several longing glances she cast at the man's back. As Victoria had given her a description of the young girl the duke had once proposed to, it took little to guess who this was.

"If you wish anything else, you need only to ask," the duke said almost coolly as he handed her a plate and stiffly took the next seat.

"Thank you," Annabelle responded automatically, catching yet another glance from the woman that the duke pointedly ignored. She took a bite of food but found her appetite had flown. She couldn't bear the almost palpable pain she felt between the two people. "Your Grace, why don't you simply—" she began, but the duke turned a warning glare on her. Annabelle hesitated only a moment before putting her plate aside in exasperation. "Oh, very well. If you are going into your Royal Duke act again, I'm leaving!"

Charles looked at her in shock as she rose. "Annabelle—"

She turned and impatiently glared at him.

"Would you mind sitting down, people are staring at us!" he gritted out.

"Whyever should I care whether these people look at me?" she snapped. "And I refuse to remain with someone so very prodigiously stupid that he will not even speak to the woman he loves!"

"Oh, God!" The duke hastily set down his own plate and took her arm.

"What are you doing?"

"Taking you outside where the whole bloody *ton* won't be listening!" he growled, fairly dragging her out to the gardens. "Now, you have something you wish to say?" he icily asked.

"Yes, I do." Annabelle matched his glare. "And you are not going to intimidate me, so you might as well quit trying. I assume that woman is your Sophia?"

"She is not my anything! She is Sophia Wellington, and as I have on a previous occasion pointed out, that is none of your—"

"I know, I know—none of my concern." She sighed, looking up at the pained fury in his face. "Oh, Charles"—she impulsively took his hand—"I cannot bear you looking so hurt. Could you not just speak to her?"

The duke looked down at her silently for a moment before he covered her hand in his. "My dear, dear sweet Annabelle, you are truly concerned, aren't you?"

"Of course I am. We are friends, are we not?"

He smiled as he drew her over to a nearby beach. "Yes, we are friends, my dear, but I am afraid you do not understand the situation with Sophia."

"Richard and Vicky have told me about you and her," Annabelle gently advised him. "I know you must have been hurt, but you still love her or it wouldn't bother you so that she has returned."

The duke sighed. "The woman accepted my proposal and then ran off and married another man, Annabelle."

"But she told you she loved you. And this other man was but a childhood friend."

"As she married him, I can only assume she lied."

"Charles, I saw the look she gave you. She is hurting

every bit as much as you are. Now didn't Richard say this all took place, what, less than two years ago?''

At the duke's reluctant nod she continued, ''And in the park the Countess Lieven said that Sophia's husband had been dead for over a year?'' She considered a moment. ''That leaves less than a year that they were married. And consumption is a degenerative disease—why, she must have known he was dying when she agreed to marry him.''

''That seems likely,'' the duke agreed, ''but I fail to see why—''

''Oh, Charles.'' She took his hands in hers. ''If there was someone—someone you loved, maybe not as a wife, but as a friend—and she told you she was dying, could you tell her you were leaving her for someone else?''

The duke looked at her in silence for some moments before he drew her against him. ''My dear little Annabelle—wherever did Richard find you?'' He smiled resignedly. ''I cannot promise the outcome, but I shall go and attempt to speak to her tomorrow.''

CHAPTER SEVENTEEN

Annabelle had been too tired by the end of the evening to much note the earl's silence as they drove home.

The following morning, however, as she skipped down in excitement for their morning ride, she was startled to find the earl quite morosely surveying the numerous bouquets that seemed to be arriving every few minutes.

"Richard, is there something wrong?"

The earl turned in surprise and carefully schooled his features. "Good morning, Annabelle. No, it is nothing—a minor problem. You seem to have been a great success last evening." Smiling, he gestured to all the flowers the servants were yet attempting to fit into vases.

"Yes, I suppose," she agreed rather unenthusiastically, and she pulled one of the cards from a nosegay. "Milfort? Oh yes, the gentleman with the shirt points so high he could not turn or lower his head. I was never sure if he was speaking to me or to the chandelier! Hmmm." She moved to a bundle of roses. "Let's see. Sothoby? I don't believe I recall—"

"That must be the new Viscount Sothoby," Richard offered.

"Oh yes, most assuredly—the new viscount. He spent

the dance telling me how the 'old fellow' had finally had the 'good grace to stick his spoon in the wall' and turn over the estates to 'new blood.' When I finally realized he was talking about his father's death, I put him down rather coldly—or I thought I did." She looked at the flowers in amazement. "Perhaps these are intended as an apology, do you think?"

The earl laughed. "Knowing Sothoby, I serious doubt it. More likely, he thought you were offering maidenly disclaimers to further capture his interest."

Annabelle looked at him aghast. "Richard, surely not! Do you know that his father died only last week?"

"Yes, I know." Richard shrugged. "It's reputed the man's already dropped a good portion of his initial bequest at White's in *celebration* of coming into the title."

"That is disgusting!"

Richard agreed with her outrage. "Shall I then assume you will not wish to receive the viscount when he calls?"

"Receive him? I don't even wish his flowers. Carol"—she called over the maid arranging flowers—"take these things out of here!"

The maid dubiously looked at the roses. "But miss, they are so lovely—"

"You may have them, then." Annabelle handed the surprised maid the bundle. "Just so I don't have to see them. Oh, wait." The earl grinned as she ripped the card off and tossed it into the fire with a small shudder.

Noting his look, she wryly commented, "Whatever is becoming of the young men of Society? Why, outside of you and Charles, I doubt I met more than two or three that seemed to have even a hare's brain." Belatedly seeing his raised brows, she quickly corrected, "I meant to say you and His Grace, of course."

Richard had idly flipped open a card he had removed from a delicate spray of irises, and after silently looking at it, handed it to her. "It would appear the duke has condoned your use of his given name." He turned and walked to the window as she read the card.

"'Thank you, my sweet Annabelle. You have given me hope. I will call on you after I have met with the party in question. Charles.'"

Annabelle smiled happily. "Oh, Richard, I wish I could tell you what happened but Char—His Grace specifically asked that I allow him to settle matters first."

"That is all right as no doubt Charles will be over shortly to advise me," he said curtly, glad that he did not have to hear Annabelle tell him of her love for his friend.

"To advise you—?" she began to question in confusion, only to be interrupted as loud voices were heard from the hallway.

"No, I won't! I hate you! You hit my sister! Rich-aard. Ann-nnie!"

Both the earl and Annabelle rushed into the hallway.

"What on earth is going on here?" Richard demanded as Mrs. Thornton released the hold she had on the struggling Terry's arm.

"These children are totally undisciplined hooligans!" the woman snapped, glaring at Terry and Thomas.

"She hit Cathy with a ruler!" Terry yelled. "Cathy didn't do anything!"

"She made Cathy cry!" Thomas's voice broke.

"Be quiet a moment." The earl gestured Annabelle to

calm them. "What is this about hitting the child, Mrs. Thornton?"

"I merely rapped her palm with a ruler, Lord Dunne," she haughtily advised. "The girl had all day to complete a lesson and has refused to even begin on it. And these two little demons attacked me."

"Cathy told you she didn't know how to subtract," Thomas accused. "You wouldn't help her and then wouldn't even allow Elizabeth."

"The child needs to do her own work."

"Cathy is only six, Mrs. Thornton," Annabelle began in fury. "She is only just now learning her numbers!"

"Annabelle, would you take the boys upstairs, please," Richard firmly intervened. "If I may speak to you in my library, Mrs. Thornton?"

Annabelle was met in the school room by Elizabeth, who was cuddling the sobbing Cathy. "Annie, that woman is a tyrant! You have got to make Richard get rid of her!"

"I know." She sighed. "Here, dear, let me see your hand."

Annabelle could not find any marks, but Elizabeth sniffed, "Well, she didn't hit her very hard, but you know how tender-hearted Cathy is!"

"What exactly happened?"

"Mrs. Thornton gave her those balls"—Elizabeth gestured to the desk—"and told her to divide them up and work these problems with them." She handed Annie a sheet with four simple subtractions. "I don't think Cathy understood, and she wouldn't even let me help her!"

"I could do it," the child protested, "but she scared

me. I forgot what the numbers looked like. I just wanted Liz to draw them for me."

Elizabeth and Annabelle exchanged a smile, just as a concerned Sarah came to the door to see what was wrong.

"Oh, Sarah, thank goodness," Annie called her in. "Would you please take Cathy and get her face washed? Maybe some cookies—?"

The nanny took the hint and smiled. "Of course, come along, sweetheart."

"Annie, we have been trying to tell you——" the twins indignantly began, but Annabelle stopped them.

"I know. Now listen, let's all sit down and calmly try to figure this out." She glanced about. "Where are John David and Cecelia?"

"They're taking naps," replied Elizabeth. "Mrs. Thornton doesn't bring them in until later."

"Oh, that's right. I suppose they dislike Mrs. Thornton as much as you?"

"Well, not quite as much," Thomas allowed. "The little kids are the only ones she even tries to teach! Annie, she just doesn't know anything."

"Now Thomas, I'm sure—"

"No, he's right, Annie," agreed Elizabeth. "At first, I couldn't believe it myself. She couldn't even name any of the Plantagenets and thought King Lear was an early French king. Why, just to test her once I was supposed to be translating a Latin lesson on Caesar's Gallic conquests and instead copied three stanzas from Macbeth—she said the work was excellent!"

Annabelle frowned. "But she came with such high references."

"The woman is stupid," Terry said curtly. "We have

tried to tell you, but you have been too busy going to balls and theaters so you can find some rich lord to marry and leave us!"

"What?" Annabelle looked at Elizabeth in confusion, but her sister refused to meet her gaze. "Would someone please tell me what you are talking about?"

Mrs. Cummings appeared at that moment. "Miss Annabelle, His Lordship wishes to speak to you in his library."

"Oh, merciful heaven. Very well. I'll finish this with you later," she told the others on following Mrs. Cummings out.

"See, she didn't even deny it," Thomas accused, venting a portion of his frustration on Annabelle.

"Thomas, now you aren't being fair." Elizabeth tried halfheartedly to defend her sister. "After all, Annabelle is a young woman. She can't help wanting to marry and have her own family."

"But we are her family!" Terry protested.

"I mean her own household and her own children. I shall want to marry and have children one day, too—" At the boys' horrified expressions, she hastened to add, "Of course, that will be years from now."

Terry sulked. "I don't want Annie to leave us. If she has to marry someone, why can't she just marry Richard and then we can all stay together?"

"Richard's our brother, silly!" Thomas advised his twin. "She can't marry her brother—" He considered a moment before turning to Elizabeth. "Can she?"

Elizabeth looked thoughtful. "Actually, that is for blood kin. And while Richard is really related to all of you—"

"You're saying she can marry him then?" Terry impatiently broke in.

"Well, I'm not sure, but I think so." Elizabeth looked thoughtful.

"Now that would be excellent!" Thomas declared excitedly. "Why, if Richard marries Annie, then he wouldn't leave either, would he?"

"You do have a good point there," Elizabeth complimented, as she had also been quite saddened at hearing of the earl's plans to return to sea.

"Yes, but did you see all those stupid flowers she got after that dance? All those lords and dukes and stuff are going to come calling. One of them could talk her into marrying him any time now," Terry warned.

"Well, perhaps we'll just have to think of some way to discourage them, until we can get Annie and Richard together, now won't we?" Elizabeth slyly suggested.

The boys looked at her with renewed admiration. "Liz, you're a right 'un!" they agreed.

Happily innocent of her siblings plotting her future, Annabelle was at that moment receiving welcome news from the earl.

"I have released Mrs. Thornton as governess." He stopped her happy response. "But not because she disciplined the children. Though I shall never condone reverting to physical punishment, I still believe a teacher should have a firm hand."

"I realize you are right, Richard. I know I have spoiled the children, especially the twins. However, I cannot help but be relieved you have released her. There was really something odd about that woman." She went on to explain what Elizabeth had told her on the lessons.

"That is one of the very reasons I did not offer her a second opportunity. I was left with the definite feeling she had even lied about having previously taught. She had no idea that Cathy hadn't learned numbers, and could not even tell me at what age she normally taught children such."

"What of her letters of reference?"

"Well, they were from some very impressive families of the nobility. Quite real, I am certain, as they were all signed and sealed. Though on thinking of it, as she herself was of a titled family, she would doubtless have friends willing to recommend her on her own word. Actually, I now suspect that rather than having been teaching for several years as she told me, she had probably only recently had to seek employment."

"That would fit," Annie agreed. "She certainly didn't have the dress or demeanor of someone who had been in service any time. Though I don't like her, I can't help but feel a bit sorry for her being put off so soon."

"You need not worry. I paid her a month's salary and offered my coach to take her wherever she wished, but she said she could have friends pick her up on the morrow." He considered a moment. "But on a new governess—that other woman I interviewed, Mrs. West I recall, did seem quite experienced, though just in village schools. What did you think of her?"

"I know she would be a perfect addition to the staff!" Annabelle assured him in pleasure.

"Very good, I shall contact the agency—"

"Your Lordship?"

"Yes, Barton?" the earl rather impatiently acknowledged the butler.

"I did not mean to interrupt, my lord, but the stable has had your mounts at the door for some time. I thought perhaps you had forgotten?"

The earl ran a distracted hand through his hair. "You are right, Barton; I fear I had. There has been so much going on this morning." He dubiously glanced at Annabelle. "Would you perhaps prefer to await Charles's arrival?"

"Oh no. I have been looking forward so much to our ride," she protested. "And after all of this, I am really in need of some fresh air! The duke won't be coming over until late afternoon at best."

"Very well," the earl agreed, thinking this was likely the last chance he would have to enjoy her company alone.

Annabelle on the graceful Arabian was every bit as delightful a picture as the earl had imagined it would be. He found himself keeping Saxon a few feet behind her simply to enjoy the vision. What a beautiful painting for over his library mantel, Richard mused before catching himself. One did not hang a painting of a friend's wife over one's mantel, only of one's own wife.

The earl felt a dreadful emptiness on the thought of Annabelle leaving him. Now wiser, he realized his previous disinterest in marriage had nothing to do with the conjugal state, merely the fact that he had never before loved someone.

"Oh no, I do believe it is going to rain." Annabelle pulled the mare back beside him with a disappointed glance at the rapidly darkening sky.

"So it is." Richard forced a lightness into his voice he didn't feel. "I expect we should head back."

The oncoming storm however moved in much more quickly than either expected, and the couple was still some distance from the house when large cold drops began falling.

"There is a small inn around the next turn," the earl called to her over the now-gusting wind. "We will stop there until all this blows over."

The swinging wooden sign over the entrance of the Bandy Cock appeared none too soon. The two galloped into the courtyard just as the rain began pelting them with a vengeance.

"Hurry and get Arabesque out of the rain, and be sure to dry her," Annabelle began advising the stable lad.

"Annie, would you please come in?" The earl laughed, grabbing her about the shoulders and propelling her into the public room. "That horse is a lot less likely to suffer from a chill than you."

"Oh dear, I have gotten rather wet, haven't I?" Annabelle giggled up at him as he brushed a strand of soaking hair from her forehead. "I must look a wretched sight."

"You look charming, regardless." The earl smiled, handing her his handkerchief. "Here, I will see if I might bespeak one of the good innkeeper's parlors, so you may have a fire by which to dry."

The innkeeper hurried up. "Milord, I am so sorry. I fear our only parlor is in use. A lord and his lady are having a private luncheon." He gestured to a side door leading from the public room.

Annabelle just then gave a slight shudder from the dampness, and Richard looked at her in concern. "Have you rooms to let here?"

"No, milord. I am sorry, we are but a small inn."

"It is really not necessary. I'll be fine, Richard—" Annabelle began.

"I will not risk you catching a cold." He turned back to the innkeeper. "Who is the lord in the parlor? Perhaps it is someone I know, and they will be gracious enough to share."

"Oh, milord! I don't think I could ask—" the innkeeper said, startled.

Richard glanced back at the soaked Annabelle. "Well, in that case, I shall." He strode to the door.

"Richard, really it is all right. I never catch cold—" Annie tried to convince him, following as the earl pushed open the door.

"My apologies, but would you—?" he began, but stopped in shock. "Charles!"

Surprised, the duke released the young woman he held. "Richard? My good fellow, have you never learned to knock?" he jovially inquired, to be met by a scathing glare.

"What are you doing here with—" Richard suddenly remembered Annabelle and tried to prevent her witnessing the scene. "Annie, do not—" But he was too late.

"Charles? Sophia!" She laughed in delight on seeing the blushing glow on the other woman's face. "Oh, Charles, does this mean that you two—?"

The earl stared in amazement as the duke happily took Sophia's hand. "Yes, my dear, Sophia has agreed to become my duchess!"

"Sophia—your duchess?" Richard began. "But what about—"

"Oh, I am so very happy for you both." Annabelle ran over and hugged the other woman. "Oh, Sophia." She finally noticed the other woman's surprise. "My apologies, I forgot you don't even know me!"

Sophia laughed. "Not formally, I fear, but Charles has told me all about you. I gather you are Annabelle."

The duke chuckled. "Indeed she is. If I may belatedly introduce my two dearest friends. Miss Annabelle Ashley, to whom I owe being reunited with you, my love." He smiled down at Sophia. "And Lord Dunne, Earl of Rothbury, Annabelle's brother." He clapped Richard on the back. "It pleases me that you two should be the first to know of our betrothal."

The earl smiled, more pleased than the duke could ever know. "I gather then that this is what you were coming over for this evening?"

"I'm sorry I couldn't tell you, Richard," Annabelle said, "but Charles insisted."

"I wasn't any too certain of how Sophia would accept my proposal," the duke confessed with a loving look down at his fiancée.

"I must admit it was certainly the last thing I expected." Sophia smiled at Annabelle. "When I saw Charles with you last night, particularly when the two of you vanished into the garden—"

The duke laughed. "Little did you know I practically dragged her out there to keep her from informing all the *ton* what an idiot I was being." He turned to Richard. "I owe you an apology, my friend. Heaven only knows what rumors I've stirred up about Annabelle with that episode. But I assure you I was in much greater danger from her than she was from me!"

Richard, in an extremely forgiving humor, assured his friend that he harbored no ill feelings concerning the matter.

"My dear, you are going to catch your death of cold." Sophia noticed Annabelle shiver. "However did you get so wet? Come over by the fire."

"Actually, that is the reason we came in. We were

caught in the rainstorm as we were out riding," the earl recalled, feeling Annabelle's soaked sleeve in concern. "I really need to get you home so you can change," he said to her.

"Take my carriage," the duke immediately insisted, pulling the bell cord. "You can send it back for us, as we planned to have luncheon before leaving, anyway. I'll see that your mounts are delivered back to the stable once this storm has passed."

Richard firmly instructed Mrs. Gavin to see that Annabelle had a warm bath, some nourishing broth, and be put into her bed for the remainder of the day.

Typically, after her bath Annabelle found she felt as good as new and quite refused the remainder of Richard's remedy.

"Now, miss, His Lordship very specifically instructed—"

"Mrs. Gavin, for goodness sakes. You know better than anyone that I never get sick." She laughed as she slipped into an old house dress. "I was just going to finish my discussion with the children."

Brit came back into the room. "Miss Annabelle, Barton asked that I advise you have several gentlemen callers awaiting you in the parlor." She glanced in horror at the gown Annabelle held. "Oh, miss! I thought I had thrown that thing away." She practically snatched it from Annabelle. "Here, now this is what you shall wear!" She selected a delightful sprigged muslin of cornflower blue.

"Gentlemen?" Annabelle sighed, automatically holding up her hands to have the dress slipped over her head. "But I was going to finish my discussion with the children. I have been rather worried about them."

"Why, the children are just fine, miss." Brit laughed. "As a matter of fact, I just saw Miss Elizabeth in her room. She was in her robe, said she had a bit of a headache and was going to lie down—but she said it wasn't anything to worry about," she quickly added. "The little ones, I believe, are being read a story by Miss Sarah, and the twins are in the parlor."

"The parlor—with the gentlemen?" Annabelle asked startled.

"Yes, miss. But you needn't be concerned. They are on their very best behavior. They heard you had callers and asked if they might go in to meet them." She chuckled. "Something about checking out how 'tulips of the *ton*' should dress!"

Annabelle laughed. "Well, that at least sounds like they aren't up to anything too awful. I suppose I should go down, then."

"Now, Miss Annabelle, I'm not letting you from this room until I fix your hair!" Brit advised.

Annie gave a resigned look at the smiling housekeeper. "Mrs. Gavin, could you perhaps let them know I will be down in a moment?"

Annabelle's callers—a viscount and two barons—were, in fact, quite impressed with her two young brothers. The twins, with proper admiration, had obligingly sought out all manner of detail on their tailors and the like from the amused lords, until Terrance, carefully watching the mantel clock, determined it time to change the subject.

He quite respectfully stood. "My lords, it is time our sister Annabelle will be coming down, and as we are aware you would most likely prefer not to have children about, we shall take our leave."

The men smiled at each other. "What understanding gentlemen you boys are," the viscount allowed.

"We just want for Annabelle to—" Terry began, but Thomas noticeably poked him in the ribs.

Curiously, the gentlemen looked at one another. "You wish what for your sister, son?" one baron questioned.

"Oh, it is nothing. Just the—best. That is what I was going to say—the best."

"The best?"

"Oh, yes, my lord. We do love Annabelle so, even though she—"

This time it was Thomas's turn to kick Terry quiet.

"Even though she what, child?" The viscount's smooth brow was fast becoming marred by a worried frown.

"It's really nothing, my lord. Nothing that need worry you. I am sure after a while Annabelle will be all right—it has, after all, been only a few years," Thomas assured the three now-frowning gentlemen.

"Uh, my boy." The baron, with a look at the others, drew Thomas over. "Now is there something you wish to tell us about your sister?"

"Annabelle is the very best sister in the world," Terry broke in. "And it's only because she is so very sweet and tender-hearted that she took—"

"Took what?" The gentlemen pressed when he paused.

"Well. She took Elizabeth's death so badly," the boy finally managed to whisper.

The lords looked at each other. "Elizabeth."

"Oh, yes. She was our—other sister," Thomas informed them with a melancholy smile.

"You poor child." The baron allowed himself a moment of presumed sympathy before quickly moving back to the worrisome topic. "And of course, Annabelle is still—sad over the death. But that does seem perfectly natural. You say it was—how many years ago?"

"Barely five," Thomas sighed with a covert glance at the mantel clock.

"It has been five years and she's still this upset?" The barons gave one another a worried look.

"Oh, yes—but I'm sure when enough time has gone by she'll at least no longer see poor Lizzie."

"See her!" The viscount's voice squeaked. "Ahem. I mean—did you say *see* her? Are you saying she sees this dead sister?"

Thomas had to strangle a giggle behind a hand ostensibly raised to wipe away a tear. "Yes, my lord. Of course. That is to say Elizabeth isn't really there—at least, I don't think so. So you needn't worry."

"Oh, no, of course not," the baron allowed, rather visibly shaken.

"Oh dear, my lords." Terry appeared to suddenly notice their concern. "I do hope you will not allow this small matter to affect your opinion of our sister," he begged. "Annabelle is really so very wonderful—and other than that little, very minor matter, she is quite normal, I assure you!"

"Well, almost," Thomas modified, just barely loud enough for the gentlemen to hear.

"Why, I do believe I hear our dear Annabelle coming now," Terry brightly declared.

"Please, you gentlemen would not mention anything about this to her? She is really so very sensitive about it all. Lord Dunne said we should never allow her to become, well, shall I say, distraught."

"Of course, we won't say a word," the viscount assured the twins as the parlor door opened.

"Annabelle." His sister looked down in amazement as Terrance came over and very gently took her hand. "May I introduce you to Viscount Barrington?"

"Now, why don't you sit here, Annabelle?" After the introductions, Thomas placed her carefully on an armchair facing the door. "I moved the tea tray, so you can reach it to serve for these fine gentlemen."

"My brothers never cease to amaze," Annabelle laughed, as the boys finally bowed out, leaving the door, of course, properly open. "Oh please, do sit down, gentlemen." She naturally gestured to the couch opposite her. "I do hope they have not been annoying?" she questioned as the gentlemen seemed to be acting a bit peculiar.

"Oh, no, Miss Ashley," one baron vehemently denied as they somewhat reluctantly seated themselves. "They have been quite—informative."

Annabelle questioningly raised her brows. "Informative?"

The viscount glared at the baron. "Yes, they have been telling us about their schoolwork."

"Of course, their schoolwork," the baron all too quickly agreed.

"Yes." The second baron nodded, smiling, and as a baleful silence fell, he awkwardly asked, "They are good students?"

"As good as young boys usually are," Annabelle brightly responded. "May I pour you some tea?"

"Thank you." They spoke almost as one, with broad smiles.

Annabelle vaguely wondered if perhaps London was becoming too inbred. They rather remarkably reminded her of the St. Claire family—in male form and without the giggles. At least these men weren't constantly watching the door, she grinned to herself, automatically glancing at the entrance behind them. Annabelle was somewhat bewildered as all three men nervously turned to follow her look.

The twins cautiously peeked through the crack along the side of the door. "Good, they all have their backs this way," Thomas observed in satisfaction. After glancing around, he gestured to their older sister hiding in the hall closet.

"Do you take sugar, my lord?" Annabelle graciously handed the viscount his cup. "You must try one of these scones—our new cook is wonderful with pastries."

The men began to relax as the lovely young lady continued a light conversation while serving them.

The second baron finally determined the gel was doubtless sane enough, at least to provide relief from his strained financial circumstances. And she was definitely a beauty. He smiled charmingly. "My dear, has anyone told you what absolutely lovely hands you have?" he began, catching her fingers as she went to reach for a scone.

"Oh, my lord, well no, as I recall." She forced a smile glancing down in amazement to see the viscount scooping up the very pastry she'd reached for. Was there a famine, or some such, in London she didn't know about?

"Lady Annabelle, I do not believe I have told you how I enjoyed our dance at Almack's last evening," the viscount quickly chimed in. Being also rather pinched of purse, he refused to let this baron get the jump on him. The wench seemed quite controllable, whatever her condition.

"Thank you, Lord Barrington." Annabelle smiled.

"I do hope you were pleased with my small offering of flowers?" The last baron didn't wish to be left out—after all, the others considered her safe enough. . . . "I don't seem to see them here," he said suddenly. "I do hope you received them—the pink roses?"

"Oh, yes, of course, my lord. The pink roses." She quickly searched for an excuse, as she didn't really recall them at all. "I put them in our upstairs sitting room. My sister does so love roses. I hope you don't mind my sharing?"

"Your—sister?" The baron stared.

"I wasn't aware you had a sister?" the viscount carefully questioned.

"Oh my, yes." Annie smiled. "Three in fact. There's Cecelia Louise. She is the youngest—just a bit over four. And there's Cathy—Catherine, I should say. She is such a dear. Just six." The lords had just begun to relax when she added, "And, of course, there is Elizabeth. She will be eleven this year."

"Elizabeth!" They stared.

"Yes?"

"Uh, this—Elizabeth—you have—seen her recently?"

Annabelle looked at him oddly. "Well, actually not today—at least so far—" Just then she caught a glimpse of something at the door and glanced up. She stared in amazement as her sister wafted by the entrance in her long white nightgown. "Elizabeth, whatever are you—?"

"What?" Tea sloshed as the lords' heads spun to stare at the now-empty doorway.

Annabelle quickly gathered some linen napkins, saying in embarrassment, "I am so sorry, it was nothing—I did not mean to startle you." She dabbed at the spilled tea. She certainly didn't care to explain that her sister was running about in the hall in her nightdress. "Please do sit back. Here, let me pour you some more tea."

"But, you saw Elizabeth—you said?"

Annabelle lightly laughed. "I was mistaken—it must have been Barton. It just—um, worried me when I thought it was little Lizzie, as she is supposed to be lying down."

The lords gasped. "Lying down?"

"Yes. Oh, you needn't look so worried, it's nothing serious. I am sure she'll be up and about again soon." She cheerfully smiled. "Would you like another scone, Baron?"

"I don't believe so." The gentleman shakily smiled. "I really think I must be going." He put his cup down and began to rise.

"Well, I am pleased you—" Annabelle glanced past him to see Elizabeth once more dreamily wandering by. Could she be sleepwalking? "Lizzie?" she called out, forgetting about the gentlemen.

She stared in disbelief as tea cups went flying as the three gentlemen leapt from the sofa.

"For heavens sakes, it is only my sister!" Her words, however, only seemed to speed them faster toward the door.

Barton moved back in shock as the lords snatched their own hats and gloves from the rack and flung open the door.

"What in the—" The earl, just returning from an appointment, found himself shoved to the side by the three lords.

"Who on earth were those men?" He turned in bewilderment to Annabelle and Barton.

"They were my gentlemen callers—just leaving." Annabelle vaguely smiled. "You know, Richard, you were right. I think I should go upstairs and lie down for the rest of the day."

The earl turned to Barton. "Do you—?"

"No, my lord," the butler ever so carefully denied.

CHAPTER EIGHTEEN

Richard was just heading for his library the following morning when a message was delivered for him. The earl frowned down at the Royal Crest of the House of Hanover, before slitting it open to read the brief enclosure.

What in heaven's name could the Prince Regent be summoning him for? Though he had in years past been friends with the young Prince, he'd opted against joining the pretentious Carlton House set once he became Regent.

Richard glanced up at the knock on his open door. "Come in, Mrs. Cummings. Did Barton not mention I requested my tea in here?" he questioned in surprise as the woman entered empty-handed.

"Tea? Milord, I believe someone else is bringing— Oh, milord, something terrible has happened! I must speak to you!"

"Good heavens, woman!" Richard stood in sudden concern. "What is it?"

"It's—the children. Oh, Your Lordship, we didn't know—we thought they were with Sarah. Oh, heavens, milord. Mrs. Gavin, she is still searching everywhere, but I fear—" Her voice broke in a sob.

"Mrs. Cummings, do calm down and tell me what has

happened." With effort he kept his own voice steady as he asked, "Now, what is it about the children?"

"They—they are gone, milord!"

"Gone! Did you say they are all gone?"

"No—no, milord. Just the two little ones. Master John David and Miss Cecelia. We thought—oh, I'm so sorry, milord, but we thought they were with Miss Sarah—and—she thought they were with Miss Annabelle—and—and nobody knows where they are."

"Richard!" Annabelle hurriedly came into the room. "John David and Ceci—"

"I know, I know." He caught her hands to quiet her. "Now let us stay calm and try to discern where they might be. You have completely searched the manor? What of the other children—have you inquired of them?"

"Yes, milord. They thought the two were with Miss Sarah as they usually are during this time of day—taking their naps."

"Where exactly is Sarah?"

"Here, milord," replied the red-eyed woman, who was just coming into the room.

"How is it that you were not watching the children, Mrs. Carstairs?" Richard demanded.

"My lord, as I told Mrs. Cummings, I thought they were still with Miss Annabelle—"

"Sarah," Annabelle broke in, "why would you think they were with me? I haven't seen them."

The nanny stared. "But miss—the governess, Mrs. Thornton, came and got them for lessons after lunch and then she said you would be taking the two of them to the park."

"Mrs. Thornton. Mrs. Thornton was released as governess yesterday."

"Released?" Sarah looked at him in horror. "But sir, no one told me."

Richard ran a hand through his hair. "I suppose we didn't. You had no way of knowing, Sarah." He comfortingly patted the frantic woman on the shoulder. "At least I suspect we know what has become of them. Though I cannot imagine why the woman would have taken them," he grimly said. "Mrs. Cummings, did anyone actually see Mrs. Thornton leave?"

"I don't know, milord. I expect maybe some of the kitchen hands. She had the carriage that picked her up pulled to the kitchen entrance to load her trunks. That's probably when she slipped the poor dears in it."

"Go immediately and bring to me anyone at all who was around when she left," he ordered.

A startled little group of kitchen help was quickly assembled in the library.

"Now, you needn't be afraid," the earl said soothingly. "I simply want to know whether any of you saw Mrs. Thornton leave today with the children."

"Oh, no, milord. We didn't see her take no children away," they protested.

"Very well, what did you see, if anything?"

After a moment of silence, a pot boy hesitantly spoke up. "Pardon me, Yer Lordship—I seen 'er leave in that fancy carriage o' th' baronet's, but mind you, I ain't seen no young 'uns—course them curtains was pulled and all—"

"The carriage of what?" Richard asked sharply.

"Why, the baronet's, Yer Lordship. Me brother, he worked for them for a while so I knows the carriage. It were the Baronet Rothschild's carriage, fair enough, what picked up that governess lady—"

"Thank you, boy!" Richard handed the delighted lad

a half-crown. "You did very well." He nodded to Mrs. Cummings to take the kitchen help back.

"Richard, what does this mean?" Annabelle frantically asked. "Who are these Rothschild people?"

The earl took her hand and led her over to the couch. "Mrs. Gavin, tell Barton to have my carriage readied immediately. If the rest of you will excuse us?"

As the door closed behind the servants, he said, "I did not tell you this before as I did not believe the woman would really do anything." Richard continued to explain about Mrs. Rothschild's relationship to the children, and the suspicions that he and the duchess had discussed.

"So she is their aunt? But she won't be able to—you won't let her—keep them?" Tears rolled unnoticed down her cheeks as Annabelle beseechingly looked up at him.

"No, my darling, I will not." Richard drew her comfortingly against him, neither of them noticing the endearment. "I am going right now to bring them back."

"Richard, let me go with you."

"Annabelle, I don't think—"

"Please, Richard. They may be frightened."

"Very well." He stood and suggested, "You run upstairs and change. We will be stopping by Carlton House."

"Carlton House?"

"Yes. I received a rather strange summons from the Prince Regent just this hour. I cannot but think it has something to do with this matter, considering Mrs. Fitzherbert's friendship with the Rothschilds."

"Lord Dunne, the Earl of Rothbury. And Miss Annabelle Ashley," the butler announced as they entered the Prince's reception room.

Entering the room, however, they found not the Prince Regent as Richard had somewhat expected, but rather Lord Kettering, one of the Prince's lesser but definitely most staid officials.

"Dunne. I have not seen you since you were a lad at your father's knee. May I extend my belated condolences on his death?"

"Thank you, sir," Richard said simply before turning to introduce Annabelle.

"Lord Kettering, may I present Miss Annabelle Ashley, my step-sister."

The gentleman but briefly bowed over her hand. "What a lovely—step-sister." Annabelle and Richard exchanged a questioning glance at the man's odd expression.

"Lord Dunne, the Prince has asked that I extend his apologies," Lord Kettering explained, appearing rather ill at ease with his duty. "He was—called away on business and requested I handle this interview for him."

The earl smiled understandingly, well aware of how the Prince often found other matters to attend to when an unpleasant audience could be handled by someone else. "Of course. I fear I must admit, however, to having no idea what this matter is about."

The lord hemmed for a moment, "Actually, sir, though the Prince generally would never involve himself in the family matters of others, I fear your household is causing some disharmony with his. It appears there is a matter of some children—"

"Lord Kettering, have you—" Annabelle anxiously began, but Richard took her hand to quiet her.

"We are very concerned at the moment on the welfare of John David and Cecelia, our brother and sister who have vanished."

"I am aware of that. They are here at Carlton House, in fact. So you need not worry. And," he added, seeing the earl's narrowing eyes, "I would like to assure you, the Prince had nothing to do with their removal from your household. In fact, he dispatched that note to you as soon as he discovered Mrs. Rothschild and the children with Mrs. Fitzherbert."

"Mrs. Rothschild brought the children to Mrs. Fitzherbert!" The earl stared in disbelief at him.

The man sighed. "It appears Mrs. Fitzherbert has, for some unholy reason, entered into a friendship with that wretched woman and, so that any of us might have another moment's peace about here, the Prince instructed that I intervene at once to settle the matter."

"Lord Kettering," Richard began somewhat coolly, "with proper respect, I must say I fail to understand what authority either Mrs. Rothschild or Mrs. Fitzherbert has to interfere in matters of my family. I certainly question their removing family members from my household."

"Normally none," the lord allowed, "however, as the matter has been brought to Carlton House—" He paused letting Richard draw the obvious conclusion. "Getting right to the matter, Mrs. Rothschild, aunt to the two children, has asked that the Prince Regent intercede in having them placed under Rothschild guardianship."

"Richard!" Annabelle turned to him in distress.

"It's all right, my dear," Richard said comfortingly to Annabelle before continuing with Lord Kettering. "Lord Kettering, this same family that now seeks guardianship was very specific in their rejection of any duties to these children upon my father's death."

"I am aware of that. It takes no untoward discernment to see into this woman's motives, Lord Dunne." The man obviously sought to soothe him. "The rumors abounded at your father's death that Rothbury carried naught but debt to its inheritors. And now, word is about that you have more than refilled the estate's coffers?''

Richard smiled at the polite question. "I have been most fortunate with my shipping interests. And in truth, the title was sufficiently entailed as to be beyond the reach of all but the most secured creditors. On the matter at hand, as the Prince must recognize this woman's motives to be of none but greed, I fail to see why any should question my guardianship. Obviously, as brother to the children, my rights stand over hers."

"Of course, at least if your household can be deemed to be a proper atmosphere for the raising of minors."

"What?" The earl stared. "Surely, sir, you are not—"

"Dunne," the lord interrupted with a glance at Annabelle. "I had not expected that—um, Miss Ashley would be at this audience. There are matters I would prefer to speak of in private. Ahem, perhaps the young lady would like to go speak to the children to reassure herself as to their welfare?"

Once Annabelle left the chamber, the lord turned to the younger man. "Please understand that as a friend of your father it truly pains me to even have to address such a matter, but as certain accusations have been made. . . ." He made a gesture of helplessness.

The earl waited in stony silence.

"I have advised the Prince how difficult it must be to manage six small children in a new household, so no credibility has been given to testimony by your late governess, a Mrs. Thornton, I believe, that the children are allowed to run wild. Actually, on having met the woman, I personally can only applaud your judgement in dismissing her. Doubtless, her testimony against you is in large measure due to her recent dismissal. At the

Prince's request, I spoke with the children themselves and am pleased to advise you that they seem more than happy in your care."

Richard sighed. "Then what—?" he impatiently began.

"I know, I know. I am dissembling like some school gel because I find this such an awkward matter. Lord Dunne, there seems to be some question on your— relationship with Miss Ashley."

The earl's face began to turn an angry red. Regardless, Lord Kettering pressed on. "Mrs. Rothschild contends that the household is an unfit one for the children to continue in, on the basis that Miss Ashley, being of no real kin to yourself, is residing with you."

"Annabelle is my step-sister," the earl gritted out, "and being a female, underage, with no other relatives or form of support, her well-being is my responsibility, as is that of her sister, Elizabeth, also of no blood kin to myself!"

"But this Elizabeth is but a child, not a beautiful young woman like Miss Ashley."

"Are you suggesting, Lord Kettering, that I am conducting an immoral relationship with my step-sister Annabelle?"

Surprisingly, the man chuckled aloud. "Though that is the accusation, frankly I had no doubt of its lack of validity. You have quite a reputation as the stickler for propriety. I well remember your father bemoaning your studiousness as opposed to your older brother. However, as you must know, in the *ton*, truth always falls to appearance, and the girl does reside with you."

"I have not only one, but two very respectable housekeepers in full residence, not to mention a nanny and until most recently Mrs. Thornton. Unfortunately, I have no adult female relatives I'm aware of to bring in, were there even room for them. Heaven only knows how the bloody gossipmongers could imagine with six children running about how anyone could possibly be—"

The lord raised an amused brow. "I do see your point. Nonetheless, the rumor is about," he added seriously. "You have to understand that the Prince has now placed the matter in my hands. Personally, on the Prince's behalf, I can not sanction the children remaining in your household without some remedy to this matter."

"Well, I suppose there must be some distant female relation somewhere I could bring in—or just move out to the club myself—"

"No, I fear it is much too late for that. As I see it, the only way to completely discredit the rumors is for one of you to marry—which perhaps is in the offing? I have heard that the Duke of Heatherton is showing a decided partiality for Miss Ashley." Lord Kettering was surprised by the man's cold glare.

"They are friends only! I expect Heatherton shall be making an announcement shortly on his betrothal, but not to Annabelle."

"Hmm," the older man continued, curious. "That must have been a disappointment to you. As Heatherton is your friend, and a duke, I would have thought it most felicitous had he made an offer for your sister."

Richard made no comment, and Lord Kettering considered him in growing concern for a moment. "Lord Dunne, you do think of Annabelle as only your sister, do you not?" Richard remained silent. "For God's sake, man, you are not allowing this woman to live with you while harboring other than brotherly emotions?"

"I have myself but recently realized that the nature of

my feelings had changed toward Annabelle," Richard uncomfortably admitted.

The older man groaned. "And may I presume the lady in question is—amenable to these changed feelings?"

"Actually, I believe she is yet unaware of them, but I do not think she will consider the change—adversely."

"May the saints preserve us!" Lord Kettering sighed. "Do you not realize the position in which this places us? The girl is obviously compromised, and as she has no relatives to act for her, her protection falls upon the Prince as Sovereign. I fear I can see nothing for it but that you must marry the girl."

"Well, I suppose if that's a royal order." The earl could not restrain a grin.

"I gather then that the idea of marriage is not overly vexatious," Lord Kettering quipped dryly as he crossed to a desk. He scrawled something on a sheet of paper and applied the royal seal. "Here, this shall serve as special license from the Prince. Please see to it that the matter is resolved with expedience in order that I'll not have to be confronted by that confounded Rothschild Goth of a woman—ever again. And kindly take your siblings with you," he added decisively. "His Majesty has been in a most foul humor all day, as Mrs. Fitzherbert has done nothing but coddle them since they arrived."

CHAPTER
NINETEEN

Annabelle was too happy to be taking the children home to even question Richard on what had transpired between him and Lord Kettering after her departure from the room.

"John David! Ceci!" The older children all excitedly ran down to meet them as they came in the door.

"I told you Richard wouldn't let anyone take them away," Elizabeth informed the twins as she hugged the two little ones.

"We got to see the Prince!" John David declared importantly.

"And his wife!" Cecelia added. "I sat on her lap and she read me a story!"

"The Prince doesn't have a wife, silly," Elizabeth informed the child.

"Does, too!" Cecelia indignantly insisted. "She told me they were married, but it was a secret so I wasn't to tell anyone." She looked at her audience a moment in worry. "But sisters and stuff don't count, so it's all right to tell you," she decided. "Where's Miss Sarah? I want to tell her about seeing the Prince." She gaily skipped off and up the stairs.

"Me, too." John David headed to the landing, and the twins and Cathy immediately joined in to make it a race.

"Well, they don't seem to have been too adversely

affected by their little ordeal." Richard grinned down at Annabelle.

She laughed. "I do believe they shall all survive. What do you suppose that was about concerning Mrs. Fitzherbert? Though she seemed such a nice lady, I was told she was but the Prince's light o' love?"

"Annabelle!" Richard indignantly looked at her. "You should not even know of such things."

"Oh, Richard! This is the nineteenth century," she archly advised him.

"What's a light o' love?" Elizabeth, who neither of them noticed having remained behind, inquired with keen interest.

"Lizzie!" Annabelle cried in shock. "You should not even know such a word!"

"But it's the nineteenth—"

"Lizzie. Go upstairs!" Annabelle demanded, avoiding the earl's eyes.

"Carol is coming with a tray, Miss Annabelle," Mrs. Gavin said as she entered. "I expect you two might be wishing for a spot of tea by now?

"Oh, thank you." Annabelle smiled gratefully. "It has been a bit of a trying day. Richard?"

"Tea would be most welcome," he readily agreed. "You may have her take it into the parlor."

Once they were settled in the parlor, Annabelle turned to Richard. "You never told me what you and that Lord Kettering discussed," Annabelle recalled as she tucked her legs comfortably beside her on the sofa.

Richard turned to contemplate the fire while he considered just how he might get around embarrassing Annabelle by letting her know of the rumors.

"Thank you, Carol." Annie smiled a dismissal to the girl. "I shall pour."

"Well?" she questioned on handing Richard his cup as he took a seat opposite her.

"Mrs. Thornton had apparently raised a number of questions on the way the children were being raised. It took little to convince Kettering of Mrs. Rothschild's motives in having that woman spy for her."

"Surely that could not have been sufficient reason for her to have taken the children and involved the Prince himself?"

"Excuse me, Your Lordship,"

"Yes, Barton." The earl was glad of the momentary interruption.

"The Earl of Stratford, sir. He is inquiring whether Miss Ashley is at home?"

Richard carefully restrained himself. "I suppose you may show the gentleman in—"

"Oh dear, must we?" Annabelle interrupted, and at his look, quickly added, "I'm sorry, if you wish to admit him—"

"There is some reason you did not wish to see Stratford? I seem to recall you spoke to him for an extended time at Almack's. Did he do something to annoy you?" Richard sharply queried.

"Oh, no. Not at all. The earl was one of the few I actually enjoyed meeting—" She hesitated. "It is just that it was so pleasant having a few minutes to ourselves," she finished, feeling oddly shy.

Richard considered her a quiet moment before smiling. "Miss Ashley is not at home, Barton."

"I have been thinking." Inspired by her words, he adroitly avoided returning to the previous subject. "Did you not say you mainly resided at the Swansea estate before your mother's death?"

"Yes. Why?" Annabelle curiously looked at him. She

was somewhat surprised at his mention of the Swansea estate.

"Did you like it there?"

Despite a sudden lack of appetite, Annabelle carefully busied herself buttering a scone. "It was quite nice." He wanted to send them away! And she had thought they had been getting along so well—even that maybe he— that was silly, Annabelle firmly told herself. Richard quite obviously just considered himself her brother.

"It occurs to me that London perhaps is not the best of areas to raise young children. I should think you would all enjoy the seaside as it soon shall be quite warm," Richard continued, considering with pleasure having her much more to himself on the huge, rambling estate.

"I am sure you are right," Annabelle bleakly agreed. Apparently this last episode had convinced him they were too much of a bother. "The children really need more room to roam."

The earl finally noticed her lack of enthusiasm for the idea. "I am perhaps being selfish," he allowed in disappointment, "as the Season has only just begun. I should not even consider taking you away from all the social events."

"No, that is quite all right. I really don't mind." Annabelle smiled a bit too brightly.

"Your Lordship?"

"Yes, Barton," the earl impatiently acknowledged this new interruption.

"I am very sorry, my lord, but the Duke of Heatherton is in your library. He said it is a matter of some urgency."

The earl looked worriedly at Annabelle. "May we continue this later, my dear? You will excuse me."

* * *

"Oh, come now, Brit," Elizabeth beseeched Annabelle's maid. "If you don't tell me I shall simply find someone else who will."

"Miss Lizzie!" The maid giggled at the young girl's persistence. "Well let me see. A light o' love is—" She sought for some explanation that would not overly endanger the child's innocence. "Actually, it is short for 'light love' or someone who is, well, loved but lightly," she tried.

Elizabeth frowned. "So if this Mrs. Fitzherbert is the Prince's light o' love, then he must just love her a little? Is that what you mean?"

"Yes, miss, that is it," the maid allowed in relief.

"But then if he only loved her lightly, why would he marry her?"

"Marry her?" The maid stared in astonishment. "Surely he didn't?"

"No, Cecelia insisted that Mrs. Fitzherbert said they were married."

"Huh," the girl sniffed. "Perhaps he was forced to or something—lord knows he has certainly compromised the poor dear!"

"Compromised? What is that?"

"That, miss, is what you must ever be on guard against when you become older!" the maid sagely advised.

"Just how shall I beware of something unless I know what it is?"

"I suppose that is a point," the girl allowed. "Well, compromised is when you allow yourself to get caught with some gentleman alone and—well, then you have to marry him."

"Marry him? Surely you jest—for simply being alone?"

"Well, alone somewhere you normally shouldn't be—uh, together. That's the rules of Society, miss," the maid said firmly, ending the conversation.

"Hmm. Have to marry him, you say," Elizabeth mused. "Brit, have you seen the twins?"

The earl managed to placate his concerned friend. "Heatherton, I truly appreciate the offer from you and the duchess to have Annabelle reside with you. I admit being surprised that the rumors have spread so quickly, but I expect quite shortly to have resolved the presumed impropriety of her living with me."

At the duke's questioning look, Richard showed him the special license.

"You're going to marry her?" Charles began in concern. "Dunne, the matter is not that serious of yet."

His friend laughed. "Heatherton, I love Annabelle."

"Love her!" The duke stared in disbelief at Richard's announcement. "Good God, man, why did you not tell me this sooner? Do you realize how close I came to offering for her myself? If Annabelle had not forced me to face my love for Sophia . . ."

"Apparently, my friend, what my Annabelle did for you, you have done for me. You see, it was not until I thought you were going to take her away from me that I faced my own feelings. I fear I had been fighting some very improper thoughts for a *brother* to be having for some time now."

The duke chuckled. "And I was so impressed at your gazing upon such a delightful beauty with none but familial concerns."

"I did try," the earl solemnly allowed.

* * *

"And so," Elizabeth assured her fellow conspirators, "all we have to do is see that they get caught alone, and they have to get married! See?"

"That is stupid," Terry snapped. "They are alone together all the time—in the library, in the parlor. Why, they were down there just a while ago having tea."

Elizabeth looked momentarily nonplussed. "Apparently then, that isn't quite enough. Well, Brit did say alone somewhere where the two of them shouldn't be."

"So how are we supposed to know where they shouldn't be?" Thomas quizzed.

"Well, I heard Mrs. Gavin get real mad at Carol because she caught her about to take Jeb in her bedroom!" Terry recalled.

"Yeah," Thomas agreed. "Maybe the bedroom is where they shouldn't be."

"That must be it," Elizabeth declared.

"Good, we must hurry. I saw another one of those dumb lord something-or-the-others at the door earlier, but I don't think Barton let him in."

"Oh, no—and I heard Mrs. Cummings say the duke is just now in Richard's library! What if he is asking Richard for Annie's hand at this very moment?" Elizabeth cried. "Does anyone know where Annie is?"

"Yeah, when I came by she was just going into her room—" Terry grinned lifting his eyebrows. "Her bedroom!"

"Perfect. But how are we going to get Richard to go to her bedroom?"

After his friend left, Richard returned to the parlor to find Annabelle gone. In a state of extreme frustration, he had just returned to his library when Terrance knocked.

The earl somewhat impatiently looked up from the papers he was reading as the twins entered. "Well, boys, what is it you need?"

"Richard, we are worried about Annie," they began, and exchanged a victory glance when the earl immediately set down the papers.

"What is wrong with Annie?" he demanded.

"I don't know. She won't tell us," Terry said mysteriously, "but I heard her tell one of the maids she felt, uh, hot—and sort of sick."

"Has Mrs. Gavin been advised?" The earl rose in concern to pull the bell rope, but Thomas quickly stepped in the way. "Oh, no sir, please! You mustn't! Annie said she absolutely didn't want either of the housekeepers to know."

At Richard's look of incredulity, Thomas hurriedly added, "She said they'd give her a purgative!" He latched on the one thing he despised most. "And you know how she hates purgatives!"

"Well, at least I can imagine," the earl allowed, smiling. "Now, I am sure Annabelle will be fine or she would summon Mrs. Gavin—"

"Please, Richard." Terry caught the earl's hand as he went to sit back down. "We're really worried—couldn't you just check on her to be sure she's all right?"

"Oh, very well. If that alone will satisfy the two of you. Come along then and we shall see to her." The earl stood and held the door for them.

The boys exchanged panicky glances. "Well, we thought we—We'll be along presently," Terry finally said. "Annie asked if we'd find her a book."

"Yes, I think she said she'd left one in here," Thomas

affirmed, wandering to a shelf. "But you hurry on up, sir, because we are real worried about her."

The earl shook his head in wonder as the boys busily began studying his library shelves. Perhaps Annabelle would know what this was all about, he finally decided with an uneasy feeling as he climbed the stairs to her room.

"Annabelle?" The earl lightly rapped on her door.

Annabelle sat up from where she had been curled in a miserable knot on the love seat staring into the fire. "Yes?"

"It's Richard. May I come in?"

"Just a moment." She shook her crumpled skirts out and carefully schooled her features before opening the door.

He looked down at her flushed cheeks in concern. "Have you a fever?" He felt her forehead.

Annabelle felt herself unexpectedly blush at his touch. "No. I'm fine. I've just been sitting by the fire." She found herself suddenly shy with him and could not meet his eyes.

At her odd behavior, Richard became truly concerned. "Come over here and let me have a look at you." He drew her over to the light. "You are warm and are quite flushed."

Annie found herself becoming even warmer and more flushed as the earl stroked her cheek and felt her racing pulse. "I'm really fine, Richard." She forced herself to move away from him and walked to the love seat. "Was there some problem Charles wished to speak to you about?" She desperately tried to change the subject.

The earl, however, wasn't fooled at all by her subterfuge. "Annabelle, my dear, I know something is wrong.

If you are not ill, then is something worrying you?" He sat beside her and took her hands. "When we were speaking earlier and I mentioned Swansea, I sensed you draw away. It is all right if you do not wish to go."

Annabelle lowered her lashes in embarrassment as she felt her eyes tear. "No, I really don't mind—if you want us to."

"Annie, Annie." He raised her chin and stared in horror as tears rolled over his hand. "Sweetheart, surely, you do not think I would force you to do anything you don't wish to? You must forgive me. I was being selfish, as I myself do not overly enjoy all this social scene. I had but thought to go somewhere quiet with you—and the children," he hastily added, "but it is perfectly understandable—"

"You're saying you would go with us?" she asked hopefully.

The earl looked down at her in surprise. "Of course, I would go with you. You thought—my dear, you thought I was sending you away?" he asked incredulously.

"We have been a dreadful amount of trouble. And now the governess—and that horrid Mrs. Rothschild—and even getting the Prince Regent involved. You wouldn't have any of those problems except for us."

"Listen to me, Annabelle." He comfortingly drew her into his arms. "These matters were not caused by any of you. It was solely a product of the Rothschilds' greed. But even had it been problems caused by the children, I would not mind solving them because that is what I am here for—I am their brother."

"But just because you are our brother—" she began, anxiously considering the buttons on his shirt front.

"Annabelle." The earl decisively raised her chin to make her look at him. "I am not *your* brother!"

She blinked. "You are not my brother?" She felt her heart pound as his fingers gently stroked her throat.

"No."

"But you just said—"

"That I was their brother." Richard's embrace ever so subtly changed. His hand entangled itself in her hair as he drew her closer. "I am their brother, but not yours. Unless, of course, that is all you would wish for me to be?"

Annabelle smiled happily as she felt his lips brush her forehead and cheek. "Well, actually I suppose I do have rather enough brothers," she managed before his mouth finally found hers.

"My darling, there are some things I haven't told you."

Some minutes later, while still holding her, the earl briefly described what had occurred in his meeting with Lord Kettering. "I didn't wish to cause you embarrassment concerning these rumors."

"Richard, do not feel you have to marry me because—" Annabelle began in distress, but he stopped her.

"I am marrying you, my love, because there is nothing in the entire world I wish to do more. And happily," he grinned, "the situation demands that I may do so with almost indecent expedience. I could not have planned it better myself had I tried!"

"Richard!" she chastised, embarrassed.

"Aha!"

Both Annabelle and the earl started as six children marched into the room.

"Annie, I must inform you that you are quite thoroughly compromised by this man!" Elizabeth decisively pointed at Richard.

"What?" The two stared in confusion at the little entourage.

"Yes, indeed, compromised," the children chimed.

"You are in your bedroom with this man alone and we have seen you!" Elizabeth solemnly continued.

"We have seen you!" the chorus happily agreed.

"So you must, of course, get married." Terrance sternly frowned at the earl. "Immediately."

"What on earth are you children—?" Annie began.

"And it doesn't matter even if the duke or one of those other dumb lords wants to marry you and take you away. You can't go because you have to marry Richard and stay with us," Thomas triumphantly added.

Annabelle and Richard looked at each other, finally beginning to understand.

"That's true!" Cathy and Cecelia giggled, climbing onto their laps. "Cause S'iety sez!"

"S'iety sez?" The earl raised a brow at Annabelle, but she merely shrugged.

"Society's Rules," Elizabeth enlightened them with a sniff. "And, Richard, it also says you can't go sailing off in your ship leaving us—uh, Annie that is. Except maybe for short voyages."

"Or you could take us with you!" John David hopefully added, confiscating the earl's remaining free knee for a stool.

"Thank you. That is very generous," the earl wryly quipped.

"So now you do understand that you have to get married?" Elizabeth questioned, somewhat worried that the two seemed to be taking their fate so well.

Richard shook his head in dismay. "Alas, I fear, Annabelle, that they have us!"

"We have you—dead to rights!" the twins decreed as, being much too old for laps, they happily flopped before the fire.

"You mean we must marry?" Annabelle asked in hushed tones.

"Aww, Annie, Wichard's weally nice," Cecelia soothingly reassured her.

Annabelle smothered a giggle. "Well, I guess if there is no way out of it."

"So when are you going to get married?" Elizabeth asked excitedly, perched on the sofa arm.

"But wait—" All eyes turned to him as Richard considered thoughtfully for a moment. Working about the various children, he managed to pull his watch from its vest pocket. "Now let's see about all this. I recall that I left the library at 5:15 P.M. Isn't that a fact?" he inquired of the twins.

"Yeah, about," Terrance cautiously agreed.

"And considering that it is now 5:55 P.M., allowing— oh, say three minutes to walk up the stairs—"

"What?" Thomas anxiously broke in, sensing something was definitely amiss.

"That leaves only thirty-seven minutes. Am I correct, Elizabeth?" he continued.

"Uh, well forty minus three—yes, thirty-seven. Why?"

"To our good fortune, my dear, perhaps there is a way out of this!" He winked at Annabelle.

"No, there isn't!" Elizabeth cried frantically, leaping to her feet. "You are compromised!"

"Oh, but I am certain—that, um, Society Rule One states quite clearly that you must be compromised for a minimum of one hour," the earl ever so seriously informed them.

"An hour!" The twins glared at Elizabeth. "You gudgeon! You didn't say it had to be for an hour!"

"Brit didn't tell me how long."

"And we, of course, must be completely alone during the hour—and here we are some"—he meaningfully glanced at the watch—"twenty-three minutes short."

"La," Annabelle sighed. "Such a pity. And I was almost resigned to the idea of being married."

The twins finally saw the light. "Come on, you buffle-heads. Let's get out of here!"

As the door slammed behind the children, Annabelle looked at the earl in some concern. "You do realize they are going to lock it?"

"Such blessed little children they are." Richard smiled, raising her lips back to his. "Ah, twenty-three minutes, alone."

"Richard?" Annabelle murmured some time later when she could again speak.

"What, my love?"

She giggled as his lips found her earlobe. "I was just thinking about those changes in Dunne Castle—"

"You were thinking about Dunne Castle?" He looked down at her, rather disconcerted.

"Yes. You do recall the old wing where the master's suite will be?"

"Yes."

"Do you remember those massive iron doors separating it from the rest of the castle?"

"Ah, the ones that you said should be removed to open the passage," he replied, smiling as he began to understand her point.

"On reconsidering, I believe you were right. Their removal would really be an unnecessary expense. Don't you think it more reasonable to merely have the lock replaced?"

"Much more reasonable, indeed," Richard chuckled as he drew her back into his arms. "And, my dear, it does please me to find that I shall have such a *reasonable* countess."

THE *NEW YORK TIMES* BESTSELLING AUTHOR OF *IMPULSE* AND *SEASON OF THE SUN*

CATHERINE COULTER

The Sherbrooke Bride

The first novel in the Bride Trilogy

Douglas Sherbrooke, Earl of Northcliffe, is a man besieged. He must have an heir. Thus he must first provide himself with the requisite bride.

Alexandra Chambers, youngest daughter of the Duke of Beresford, has loved Douglas Sherbrooke since she was fifteen. Unfortunately, it is her sister, the incomparable Melissande, he wishes to wed.

But Douglas finds himself wed to the wrong sister. If having an unwanted wife isn't enough, he is also plagued by the Virgin Bride, a ghost that is reputedly seen on the estate—and in the countess's bedchamber!

___ 0-515-10766-2/$5.99

For Visa, MasterCard and American Express orders ($10 minimum) call: 1-800-631-8571

FOR MAIL ORDERS: CHECK BOOK(S). FILL OUT COUPON. SEND TO:

BERKLEY PUBLISHING GROUP
390 Murray Hill Pkwy., Dept. B
East Rutherford, NJ 07073

NAME_____
ADDRESS_____
CITY_____
STATE_____ZIP_____

PLEASE ALLOW 6 WEEKS FOR DELIVERY.
PRICES ARE SUBJECT TO CHANGE WITHOUT NOTICE.

POSTAGE AND HANDLING:
$1.50 for one book, 50¢ for each additional. Do not exceed $4.50.

BOOK TOTAL	$_____
POSTAGE & HANDLING	$_____
APPLICABLE SALES TAX (CA, NJ, NY, PA)	$_____
TOTAL AMOUNT DUE	$_____

PAYABLE IN US FUNDS.
(No cash orders accepted.)

JILL MARIE LANDIS
The nationally bestselling
author of <u>Rose</u> and <u>Sunflower</u>

____JADE 0-515-10591-0/$4.95
A determined young woman of exotic beauty returned to San Francisco to unveil the secrets behind her father's death. But her bold venture would lead her to recover a family fortune—and discover a perilous love....

____ROSE 0-515-10346-2/$4.50
"A gentle romance that will warm your soul."—**Heartland Critiques**
When Rosa set out from Italy to join her husband in Wyoming, her heart was filled with love and longing to see him again. Little did she know that fate held heartbreak ahead. Suddenly a woman alone, the challenge seemed as vast as the prairies.

____SUNFLOWER 0-515-10659-3/$4.95
"A winning novel!"—**Publishers Weekly**
Analisa was strong and independent, Caleb had a brutal heritage that challenged every feeling in her heart. Yet their love was as inevitable as the sunrise...

____WILDFLOWER 0-515-10102-8/$4.95
"A delight from start to finish!"—**Rendezvous**
From the great peaks of the West to the lush seclusion of a Caribbean jungle, Dani and Troy discovered the deepest treasures of the heart.

For Visa, MasterCard and American Express orders ($10 minimum) call: 1-800-631-8571

FOR MAIL ORDERS: CHECK BOOK(S). FILL OUT COUPON. SEND TO:	POSTAGE AND HANDLING: $1.50 for one book, 50¢ for each additional. Do not exceed $4.50.
BERKLEY PUBLISHING GROUP 390 Murray Hill Pkwy., Dept. B East Rutherford, NJ 07073	**BOOK TOTAL** $____
NAME_____	**POSTAGE & HANDLING** $____
ADDRESS_____	**APPLICABLE SALES TAX** $____ (CA, NJ, NY, PA)
CITY_____	**TOTAL AMOUNT DUE** $____
STATE_____ZIP_____	**PAYABLE IN US FUNDS.** (No cash orders accepted.)
PLEASE ALLOW 6 WEEKS FOR DELIVERY. PRICES ARE SUBJECT TO CHANGE WITHOUT NOTICE.	